Maiden Rock Mistress

ISBN:978-1-935188-05-6

Library of Congress Control Number
LCCN: 2009928434

Edited by Star Publish
Cover by Richard Stroud from strouddigitals@aol.com
Interior design by Alicia McMullen

A Star Publish LLC Publication
www.starpublishllc.com
Published in 2009
Printed in the United States of America

I dedicate Maiden Rock Mistress to my dear friend, Barbara Williamson-Wood, a Native American who lived by the land she loved. She was an immense help in my research into the ways of the early Sioux/Lakota Indians in the area. She lost her battle with cancer in early 2009, but she left her mark on everyone she touched.

It is also dedicated to the wonderful Sugar Loaf bluffs that I enjoyed as a child when my Great Uncle Glen Bowen would take us up there. Sadly, they have also disappeared. Oh, the bluffs remain, but all of the beautiful multi-colored sand is gone, but not forgotten by those of us who got to enjoy it.

Maiden Rock Mistress

Janet Elaine Smith

A Star Publish LLC Book

CHAPTER 1

Violet Seymour lay on her bunker on the river boat as it wound its way northward up the mighty Mississippi. The constant flip-flop of the paddle wheel calmed the butterflies in her stomach. Soon it would be daybreak, and the captain had said they should arrive in Lake City in the early morning hours. Her whole future stretched out ahead of her.

Her future. She wondered if it would be as exciting as she imagined. It was just barely two weeks since she had finished her normal training, making her a full-fledged teacher. Now she had her first job, and here she was, embarking on an adventure beyond her wildest hopes.

She carefully reached inside the bodice of her dress and took the letter out. She squinted in the darkness, trying to make out the words. She wondered, as she unfolded the fragile paper, already worn from the countless times she had opened and closed it, why she even bothered. She knew every word by heart.

"My dear friends," the letter began. "Uncle Lath and I have found the Garden of Eden. Never has there been a place equal to Lake City, Minnesota. Uncle Lath built a ferry, and together we run it back and forth between Lake City, Minnesota and Maiden Rock, Wisconsin. The water on the lake is as blue as the clearest sky, sparkling and bright. As you look up at the high bluffs on every side, the brilliant colored sand seems to create its own rainbow."

She held the letter close to her heart. Such beautiful words; they were like poetry, even though they didn't rhyme. She pondered the mysterious Denis McLeod, the author of the letter. Was he as gentle and tender as he seemed? Too good to be true, she thought.

She shook her head, trying to rid her mind of such silly thoughts. A mosquito buzzed around her head, as if to help her concentrate on something besides Denis McLeod. Anything but Denis McLeod.

She was a mere nineteen years old. She had plenty of time for love and romance. Besides, Denis McLeod was a complete stranger to her. Oh, yes, her Uncle King Smith had known his Uncle Lathrop McLeod for years. Maybe she was overly anxious because so many of her friends in Morris, Illinois, where she had lived most of her life, were getting married. It was almost like an epidemic. Was she afraid of being a spinster at her young age?

"We have only two minor shortcomings in Lake City," he wrote. "There is no honest-to-goodness schoolmarm, and we need one real bad. Perhaps, if you decide to come join us, you could persuade a teacher from Morris to accompany you."

It was a wonderful invitation, especially since Uncle King and Aunt Caroline, who had raised Violet since she was only three years old, quickly decided to pack up everything they owned and head for the "Promised Land." Little Henry, their six-year-old, would be one of her first students at the new school. She wondered how many others there would be. She knew she couldn't count on Aunt Caroline to help her if she needed; Baby Palmer would keep her busy.

Lath McLeod promised Uncle King in his letter that there was plenty of land for everyone just for the asking. And Uncle Alonzo, who lived just across the lake in Wisconsin, had been trying for nearly two years to persuade the rest of the Keith clan to join him.

Violet continued reading. This was where it got so confusing. Denis McLeod seemed so pure, so wonderful. Then he was like a different person. Like good and evil, day and night, hot and cold.

"The only other drawback to this place is the Indians. 'Dakotas,' they are called. They are savages. Terrible wild creatures. If only there was some way to rid us of all of them, but such an effort would certainly lead to war. Our only hope is that if we get a real teacher, maybe they can help civilize the creatures, although I sincerely doubt that such a thing is possible."

Violet shivered, in spite of the warmth of the summer. Countless times Grandpa Benjamin told stories about his own father fighting the Indians in Vermont. They destroyed entire families, burning their homes and even killing women and children. Maybe Denis McLeod was right; maybe they weren't even human beings. She wasn't sure she was up to such a challenge, but she had to try. It was too late to back out now. She had already sent a letter of acceptance to Mr. McLeod. Still, she reminded herself, they were people, and they deserved a chance to prove themselves too.

She folded the letter and returned it to the inside of her dress, once again placing it inside her chemise. The thrill of the unknown caused her heart to skip a beat. Or was it the writer, with his flowery flowing words?

"What a foolish idea!" she scolded herself. Denis McLeod was no more interested in her—as a woman—than anything. He wanted her for her mind, nothing more. He needed a good schoolteacher for the children in Lake City, and she just happened to be the most available one. He didn't even indicate in his letter if he expected a man or a woman. She hoped she wouldn't disappoint him.

Try as she might, she couldn't shake the idea that there might be something more to it than he let on. After all, Lake City was a new town. The choice of single, available women was probably pretty slim, but she would not be a prize for some game he had in mind. No, she was going there on business. She had a job to do, and that was all there was to it.

She conjured up a mental picture of Denis McLeod. She knew he must be a Scotsman; his name told her that much. Even though her name was Seymour—a very English name—she was half Scottish herself, her mother being a Keith.

Her mind wandered to her mother and father. The trip the entire Keith family took years ago from Vermont to Illinois had been one wrought with hardship. Both her mother and father died on the journey. Violet was too little to really remember them, although Aunt Caroline had done a wonderful job of telling her so many stories about them that she felt like she knew them, even if her memories were secondhand.

Denis McLeod must have red hair, she reasoned. Every true
Scotsman she had ever seen had red hair. Of course, most of the
Scotsmen she had seen were her own relatives, but surely if they
were all redheads most other Scotsmen must be redheads as well.
He probably had a beard. He was a sailor, and every sailor she
had ever heard tell about had a beard. Oh, yes, and a curved stem
pipe, and he no doubt wore one of those silly flat captain's hats
perched askew on his head.

She laughed in the silence of the night. I'll just bet, she thought,
that he imagines himself to be a great sea captain sailing across
the wide oceans when he sets sail on little Lake Pepin. Such a silly
fool. He probably had visions of grandeur, while in reality he was
simply a delivery boy from one state to another across a lake you
could see both sides of.

She heard one of the other members of the group stirring. She
closed her eyes, pretending to be asleep. She certainly didn't want
anyone to know about her wild thoughts. She hardly dared admit
them to herself. Remember, she reminded herself, he wants you
for your brains. The rest of you is of no consequence at all.

~*~

Violet climbed up onto the deck of the riverboat as it smoothly
glided over the glistening blue-green water. She knew the current
on the river was strong, but with no wind at all it seemed as still
as the air. It is almost, she thought as she watched the trees and
shrubs on shore, as if they are moving and we are standing still.
She looked up at the clouds. The sky was a lush shade of orange
as the sun rose. She studied it, etching it in her mind, as it changed,
moment by moment, to red and yellow. She wanted to capture it
forever.

I wonder if Denis McLeod has any idea we are this close to
Lake City, she thought. She instinctively placed her hand to her
bosom, where his letter of invitation was safely tucked away—
next to her heart.

She lightly slapped her own face, embarrassed at the direction
her mind was wandering. She had to get over this silly notion she
had before they arrived. If she didn't, she was sure she would make

a first-rate fool of herself. She was as transparent as a drop of morning dew on a leaf.

She stood quietly, myriads of thoughts and ideas swirling around in her head. She tried to imagine what her school would be like. How many children would there be? Would the parents all be supportive, or was this just a whim of Denis McLeod's? Did they have a special school building? If not, where would she hold the classes? Did any of the children have any learning at all, or would she have to start with the same basics for teenagers as well as the six-year-olds?

Suddenly, in her mind's sight, a figure appeared. She envisioned a small log building, with children running to and fro in the yard, and a strong, muscular man—boasting a full head of red hair, a red beard, a captain's cap and a long-stemmed pipe, its smoke winding up into the chill of autumn air. She knew, immediately, who he was.

She smiled, not sure if she was dreaming or awake, as she watched him carry the load of wood in his arms to the side of the schoolhouse and stack it neatly. The children skipped merrily over to him, begging him to give them a ride on the ferry.

"Not now," he said, his voice deep and resonant. "On Saturday, when you don't have school. Miss Seymour wouldn't like you skipping out on your classes."

She swayed to the side, nearly losing her footing as the boat swerved. At least, she realized, she was awake. It wasn't a dream. A fantasy, perhaps, but not a dream. She could hear the clap, clap, clap of the paddle on the riverboat as it pushed them on their way to the place Denis McLeod called "heaven on earth."

She jumped when little Henry spoke. She hadn't seen him come up behind her.

"We're gonna be in Paradise today, Violet," he said.

"Yes, we are," she said, smiling at him. "Only it's called Lake City, not Paradise."

"I know that," Henry said. "But Denis said in his letter that it was like the Garden of Eden. That's Paradise, you know. Ma's told me that story lots of times."

"Yes, he did," Violet agreed. "We'll have to wait and see for ourselves when we get there."

"It's really funny, you know," Henry said.

"What's funny?" Violet asked.

"That letter. Pa kept Lath's letter, but he couldn't find the one from Denis at all. He looked high and low for it, but he said the wind must of blowed it away."

"Must have blown," Violet corrected, touching her hand to her bosom where the letter was still carefully guarded. They didn't need the letter. After all, it was meant for her. It was her invitation to a new life.

Soon everyone was stirring and the tension was high at the prospect of arriving at Lake Pepin. For some of the passengers there was nothing new about this ride at all. They were going on business, or to visit family or friends, but for others, like Violet, it was the beginning of a brand new adventure and there was uncertainty as to what they would find when they arrived, but great hope and expectation as well.

True to his word, in less than an hour the captain bellowed "Lake City ahead!"

Violet hurried to the opposite siderail with the others, anxious to see if it was everything Denis McLeod promised. She gasped, her breath catching in her throat. It was all he said, and more. The bluffs rose on all sides of the lake, creating a haven of solitude, oblivious to the rest of the world. Just as Denis had said, the sand on the bluffs was brightly colored, creating their own rainbows towering above the water. The reflections bounced back at them, making it seem like they really were in their very own Paradise.

As the boat pulled in toward the shore, the captain slowly steered it alongside a long pier. A black haired, clean-shaven tall, slim man reached out to help guide it, then fastened a chain around a high post on the dock.

Violet reached down and smoothed her long dark brown cotton skirt. She wished she hadn't been trapped in the same outfit for days—and nights. She must look a mess. In a frustrated effort to improve her disheveled appearance she grabbed at her hair, forcing it back into place the best she could. At least, she thought with relief, Denis McLeod isn't here to meet us.

One by one the passengers climbed off, carefully setting foot on the pier and then hurrying to dry ground. When it was Violet's turn, she reached up to grab hold of the captain's hand, which had been available for each one, and lifted one foot firmly onto the dock. Just as she got ready to step out the rest of the way a gust of wind charged at them and the boat blew out into the lake just far enough for Violet to fall into the water between the boat and the dock.

Splash! They all gazed in amazement as Violet disappeared, then bobbed up and down. In an instant the tall dark man threw off his jacket and plunged in after her.

Violet, when she realized what had happened, began to swim frantically towards shore, but she felt a hand grasp her around her neck.

"Hang on," the deep voice commanded. "I'll get you there safe and sound."

Violet kicked at him frantically. She was so embarrassed she wished she could stay under the water until everyone was gone. She wanted so desperately to make a good impression on the people of Lake City. Now she wouldn't dare face any of them.

She slapped at her skirt, which ballooned up around her on the surface of the water.

"Don't fight me!" the man ordered. "It isn't that far to shore."

Finally giving in, Violet settled back and let the stranger rescue her. Not that she couldn't have managed perfectly well without him, but if he thought she was some helpless little female... Well, let him think what he wanted to. He probably wasn't anybody important, anyway. For all she knew, he probably hated children!

The man helped her to her feet when the water was shallow enough for them to stand in. He grasped her elbow firmly, steadying her as she stumbled onto the sandy beach.

"And you are..." he asked as they walked along, leaving a trail of water to mark their steps.

"Violet Seymour," she answered shyly. She wished she could go back on board the boat and start all over again, but it was too late for that.

The man threw his head back, his wet dark black hair trailing down his back. He laughed, a hearty guttural laugh. He stretched his hand out towards her.

"Denis McLeod," he said. "Pleased to make your acquaintance, ma'am." He looked at her long and hard, then smiled. "Do you always enter with such a splash?" Then he laughed that same deep laugh again.

As they walked along, Violet did not dare look at him. He was not at all like she had imagined him, but he was true to his letter. He was kind enough to jump in and rescue her, yet cruel enough to laugh at her, mocking her. Two different people rolled up in one. Like good and evil. Like day and night. Like hot and cold.

"I think the children will like you just fine," he said, smiling warmly at her as they walked through the main street of Lake City like they owned the town. "I think they'll like you mighty fine."

CHAPTER 2

Violet walked into Browns' Hotel, her head firmly planted downward, with Denis McLeod's hand grasping her elbow as if she was as normal looking as anyone you might see anywhere in Lake City.

"I'd like you to show our new schoolmarm to her room," Denis instructed the gray-haired man at the desk.

Violet cringed. She hated that word: schoolmarm. She was a schoolteacher, and Mr. McLeod should know that if he had any kind of learning himself.

The desk clerk was dressed to the hilt, with a fine black suit, crisp white shirt and black cravat. His perfect appearance made Violet more conscious than ever of her own unkempt look.

He quickly put his hand to his mouth, trying to conceal his snickers, but his efforts were futile.

"This is our new schoolteacher?" he asked when he regained his composure enough to speak.

Violet could just about imagine the thoughts that must be running through his mind. She glanced at Denis, then realized that he looked every bit as wet and disarrayed as she did. At least, she thought, if the clerk thinks we went swimming together he can certainly tell we weren't skinny dipping!

He thumped loudly on the bell. A young boy came running from another room.

"Yes, sir?" he asked very politely.

"Would you please see Miss Seymour up to her room? It's…"

"I know which one it is, sir," the boy said. He turned to look at her, then asked in surprise, "You're going to be our new teacher?"

"I'm afraid so," she said, apologizing for the way she looked. "I think you will have to teach me a thing or two also. You see, I'm not much accustomed to large river boats, nor the winds which blow about on Lake Pepin."

"You fell in the drink?" the boy asked, obviously amused.

"Yes, I must admit that is exactly what I did."

"Good!" he exclaimed, nearly jumping up and down with glee.

"I don't rightly see how that can be good," Violet said, failing to see anything humorous about the situation at all.

"Oh, but it is. Don't you see? If you fell in the lake, and everyone saw you, or at least those who didn't see you I'm sure have heard about it by now, that means that you aren't perfect. I hate perfect teachers. At least those who try to act like they're perfect. You falling in the lake—that shows that you aren't any better than the rest of us. Well, maybe you're better, but you're not any smarter... Well, maybe smarter, but not..."

"James!" the desk clerk barked at the boy. "You will show Miss Seymour to her room?"

"Yes, sir. Right away, sir. This way, ma'am."

He skipped up the steps ahead of Violet, then turned around to make sure she was following him. They disappeared down the hallway to a room way at the end.

"Pa, he thought this would be quietest for you," the boy said, "so you can study and grade papers and stuff like that, you know. Teacher stuff!"

The boy chattered on gaily, nonstop, as they went inside the room. Violet looked out to make sure Denis hadn't followed her. She had seen about as much of Denis McLeod as she cared to for the present, and he had seen entirely too much of her, what with her skirts floating clear up on top of the water and his hand wandering around on her bloomers. Maybe it was purely accidental, but his hand had no business there. She told him she could make it to shore by herself.

It suddenly registered that this boy had called the desk clerk "Pa." He had been so prim and proper with him, she never imagined the man to be his father.

"The man at the desk is your father?" she asked.

"Yes, ma'am. He's my pa. He's the desk clerk, the owner of the hotel and just about the most important man in town. He's Thomas Brown, he is, and he's my pa."

Violet smiled at the lad. He was undoubtedly very proud of his father. She wondered if Thomas Brown was truly "about the most important man in town" to everyone, or just to his son.

A young girl knocked on the door, even though it was open.

"Miss Seymour?" she asked.

"Yes," Violet answered.

"Denis...I mean Mr. McLeod...says he'll be back in an hour to fetch you for supper." She didn't wait for an answer, but turned to the boy and said "Pa wants you downstairs. They've just brought Miss Seymour's bags in and he wants you to fetch them up to her."

"You bet," he said, scurrying off to get her things.

Violet made a mental note that this girl and the boy were apparently brother and sister, since they both called Thomas Brown "Pa."

"What's your name?" Violet asked the girl, but she saw that she had already disappeared in the brief moment that she had turned her back to look out the window.

Just a few minutes had passed when James came back to the room, dragging Violet's heavy bags along on the floor behind him. Violet had not closed the door, but the lad, like his sister, knocked anyway.

"Come on in," Violet said, smiling at his obvious good breeding.

He deposited the bags on the floor inside, then turned to leave.

"I wouldn't be late if I was you," James said. "Mr. McLeod, he don't take to people makin' him wait."

Violet said a soft "Thank you," but she thought that Denis McLeod had no right to make any demands on her, yet he had already ordered her to be ready for supper in an hour. Just because it was his doing to give her a job, she wasn't about to be beholding to him. She was here because of him, but she could handle her own affairs now. She would prove that to him—and to everybody else.

The thought of good food made her stomach put up a large most unladylike growl, as if defying her stubborn independence. She pushed on it, trying to quiet it. Her hand, as she pulled it away, was damp. She hurried to close the door, latching it securely against any intruders, and shed her still-wet clothing. She pulled and tugged at one of her bags, hefting it onto the bed. She took out some of the contents and looked at them.

"What am I going to do to these?" she asked herself. "There's nowhere here to heat the flatirons." She removed her wet clothing and sat on the edge of the bed. As she untied her camisole, the letter fell onto her lap. She picked it up to read it, but the ink was nothing but a series of streaks and smudges.

She looked around the room, carefully surveying it for the first time. There was a dresser, a small armoire, a bed, a washstand with a beautiful china basin and pitcher, and a thundermug. Over in one corner was a small pot-bellied stove, with a stoker leaned up against it, and a bucket of coal. It would provide more than ample heat for the small room in the cold of winter, but it would be overwhelming to start a fire in it in the dead of summer.

She turned to her bags and selected a soft gray dress with a Puritan-style collar, and tried to smooth it out as best she could with her hands. She took her fingernails and ran them over the tiny hand-stitched tucks on the front of the bodice. She smiled, pleased with her own handiwork. Aunt Caroline had taken great care in teaching her stitchery when she was just a small girl. Now, her entire wardrobe consisted of tailored, well-constructed practical garments which would hold her in good stead as a teacher. She would look the part, even though it was her first real job.

She shook her head in despair, but decided it would have to do for the time being.

She carefully stepped into a camisole and her full white cotton petticoat. Her body, which boasted a perfect form, did not need the support of a corset, although Aunt Caroline constantly chided her about not donning such a garment. The dress, even though extremely plain, did nothing to hide her curves. The waist was tight-fitting, and her bosom filled the bodice to perfection.

She walked to the dresser, standing in front of it to survey her appearance. The fabric stretched to its fullest, making the wrinkles disappear. She smiled, pleased with her looks. If Mr. Denis McLeod was going to accompany her to supper, at least she would look presentable this time.

Her mind flashed back over the past few days. Her bones and muscles ached from the long, tedious ride, first in the wagon to the river, and then on the riverboat. She certainly would not have made a first impression the way she did if she had had a choice, but one thing was certain, no one was apt to forget the day Miss Violet Seymour hit town!

She looked longingly at the soft featherbed. If she wasn't so hungry she would make her apologies to Denis McLeod and stay right there, where she could get a good night's sleep.

"Enough time for that later," she said, then shook her head, amazed that she had been reduced to talking to herself. She was accustomed to lots of activity around her, with the Keith clan—Uncle King and Aunt Caroline and little Henry and Palmer and Grandpa Benjamin and Grandma Sarrah—always present. The loneliness of being on her own, even if there were other tenants in the hotel, suddenly hit her.

"And I thought this would be so wonderful," she grumbled. In less than one day she had ridden up a river, fallen in a lake, made a complete fool of herself in front of half the town and agreed to go to dinner with a total stranger. At this rate, what could the future possibly hold that would be more exciting and adventurous? If it got much livelier than this she wasn't sure she could handle it.

She heard a loud shuffling out in the hall and opened the door a crack to see what was happening. She was just in time to see Uncle King, Aunt Caroline and the boys head for their room.

"Pa, I can't get it there," Henry yelled.

"Just kick it," Uncle King said, already loaded down with three big bags of their belongings. Aunt Caroline had her hands full carrying Palmer and his gear.

Palmer let out a wail as if to say, "I want a chance to speak my piece too."

"Ouch!" Henry yelped, stopping to rub his foot. "What did you do, fill this thing with gold?"

"Sure," Uncle King said laughing heartily. "Fool's gold!"

"I ain't nobody's fool," Henry said, stomping his good foot.

"I'm not," Violet called out into the hallway, correcting Henry. "Child, you'll never learn, will you? You need to set an example for the other children."

As Henry tugged and dragged the trunk, he slammed the door to their room shut, sticking his tongue out at her as he disappeared inside.

Violet had not given any thought to where they would live. In Illinois they had their own small, cozy home, but now they had to start over from scratch. It was, she realized, a real sacrifice for all of them. Was this what people meant by the pioneer spirit? It was a wonder any of them survived. At least the weather was nice, and she was sure they would have their own homes long before winter set in. Uncle Alonzo, who lived just across the lake in Maiden Rock, Wisconsin, was a first-rate carpenter and he had promised in every letter he had written that if they would come to join him he would help with the building.

Would she, she wondered, move in with them? Or would she be better off, now that she would have an income of her own, staying here in the hotel? As James had pointed out, it would be a quiet place to do her teacher stuff.

Her thoughts were interrupted by the Brown girl's appearance at her door.

"Mr. McLeod is waiting for you downstairs," she announced. She studied Violet carefully, then said shyly, "You look real pretty, Miss Seymour."

"Better than when you first saw me?" Violet asked, trying to put the child at ease. There was no doubt about it, Violet was a natural for a teacher; children all responded to her immediately.

"Yes, ma'am," the girl said, then hastened to add, "Course you looked pretty then too." She grabbed Violet's hand and swung it back and forth, up and down, as they walked towards the stairway together.

"Pretty wet!" Violet said, laughing.

"Well, yes," the child agreed, "but you couldn't help it the wind blew when it did."

"You're right," Violet said, suddenly feeling much better. It wasn't her fault she fell in the lake.

"What is your name?" Violet asked the girl, this time when she was still there to hear the question.

"Margaret," she replied. "'Cept most everybody calls me Maggie. Maggie Brown, that's me." Her face lit up with a big grin. "You don't need to tell me your name. I already know it. We've all been waitin' for Miss Seymour to arrive. We need a school, you know."

"Every town needs a school," Violet said, "and I'm proud to be your very first school teacher."

"Well, almost first one," Maggie said. "Reverend Hazlett, he's been tryin' to teach us, but he's not so good. Pa says it's 'cuz he's got no patience, but that doesn't make any sense to me. I thought it was Doc Vilas who had patients, not teachers."

Violet laughed at the girl. Yes, she could see that she had her work cut out for her. One of the first lessons would be to teach Maggie the difference between patience and patients.

As they neared the bottom of the steps, Violet eyed Denis McLeod. He looked extremely dapper, clad in a pair of brown tweed trousers, a sharp white starched shirt and a deep forest green velvet cutaway jacket. She stood, staring at him. He looked like he was from some faraway fairytale land, not a man who belonged in the middle of a new frontier. He turned to look at her as soon as he heard her voice.

"Good evening, Miss Seymour," he said, tipping his hat to her and bowing slightly. "My, but I have never seen anyone accomplish so much in just one short hour!"

Violet felt the heat rise in her cheeks, causing them to turn a bright crimson that closely matched her hair.

"Thank you, Mr. McLeod," she said, walking towards him.

He extended his arm for her to grasp. She hesitated, not wanting him to think that either she was dependent on him or that she was his possession.

Slowly, she put her hand through the crook in his arm, mainly for security. She felt like her knees might give out at any moment, and she didn't want to fall flat on her face—or her fanny—after the performance she had given earlier in the day.

"The dining room is this way," he said, pointing to a set of huge, heavy wooden doors. "I would imagine that you are hungry. You've had a long ride on the riverboat, and the food is never the most sumptuous fare."

Violet was surprised by Denis's vocabulary. She didn't know what she had expected, but somehow she imagined that a man in the wilds of Minnesota, a newly settled territory, would be somewhat hampered in his education. Denis McLeod was quite obviously as well-bred as anyone she had ever met. She wondered how long he had lived here, and where he had come from. One thing was certain; he didn't fit the picture she had conjured up when she was back in Illinois. No, she had barely met Denis McLeod and already he had proven to be a man of great surprises.

He pulled one of the doors open, and Violet stared in amazement. The dining room was filled with square tables, each one covered with crisp white table linens and topped with assorted jars and bottles holding brightly colored wild flowers. There were people sitting at several of the tables, mostly men, with a few couples scattered throughout. None of them, she noticed, were dressed at all like Mr. McLeod; their clothes were simple country styles.

"Evenin', Mr. McLeod," a woman said as they entered the dining room. Violet smiled at her, even though she didn't fully understand why. She was a short woman, with her hair pulled severely back into a bun at the nape of her neck, but the few wisps of hair which insisted on falling free in curls around her face seemed to indicate that she was not what she appeared. "Your usual table?" she asked.

"Yes, Mrs. B," Denis replied. He followed her to a spot right in the center of the room, with Violet still firmly attached to him at the elbow.

"Miss Seymour," he said, pulling a chair out for her.

"I'll be back in a few minutes," the woman said, handing a carefully hand-lettered menu to each of them.

"Mrs. B," Denis said quietly, cricking his finger for her to come closer to him.

She bent down and Denis whispered something in her ear.

"Be right back," she said, grinning knowingly at them as she disappeared.

"What was that all about?" Violet asked.

"Nothing much," Denis answered, smiling warmly at his dining partner. "I just asked her if she could bring us something special."

"Special?" Violet asked.

"Yes," Denis said. "I figured this is a very special day. It's the first time Lake City has ever welcomed a brand new teacher." He focused so intently on her that Violet was afraid he would bore a hole right through her. "And a fine-looking one too, I might add."

Violet shivered slightly, her nervousness all too apparent, in spite of the warmth of the room. How much had Uncle King told Lath McLeod and his nephew, Denis, about her? She hoped she could fool them, at least for awhile, into thinking that she had some teaching experience. She felt uncomfortable, sensing that her life was an open book to her new employer.

The woman soon reappeared, carrying a bottle of red wine. She set it on the table, pried the cork out and poured some of it into two fine crystal goblets that looked like they had come straight from Paris.

"To Lake City's first and finest school and its new teacher," he said, raising his glass in the air.

Violet sat, innocently, watching him. She did not follow suit, did not clink glasses, but merely lifted the sparkling red liquid to her lips and took a big drink.

She shook her head, blinked her eyes and began to cough. Never had she known such a sensation. She felt all tingly inside, clear down to her toes. She couldn't tell for sure if it was from the wine or from Denis McLeod's presence, but it was definitely a new experience.

Denis leaned back on his chair, tipping it so the two front legs were supported only by air, threw his head back and laughed as he slapped his leg several times with his open hand.

"Well, little lady," he said between guffaws, "you passed the first test."

When she had caught her breath enough to speak Violet asked, "First test? What first test?"

"Well, we want a good moral woman for teaching the children, and from the look on your face when you drank that alcohol I can see you sure aren't a winebibbin' hussy. No, just as I suspected, Miss Violet Seymour, you are a good upright woman."

Violet was dumbfounded. The only words she could find to say were "Thank you, Mr. McLeod." Then she puzzled over how many other tests he had planned for her, and what they were supposed to prove.

"Denis, ma'am," he said, gently setting his hand on hers.

"And I," Violet said sternly, "will remain Miss Seymour!" Her mouth remained straight, yet her eyes sparkled as though smiling on their own. "For the children's sake, of course."

CHAPTER 3

Violet fell onto the soft plush featherbed in her room back at Browns' Hotel. It felt so-o-o good after the hard ground and the cots on the riverboat. Her body longed for a good night's sleep, but her mind was a whirling tornado of thoughts.

She closed her eyes, but she still saw him. He was the most arrogant, egotistical man she had ever met. He had taken great delight at the hotel in introducing her to the townspeople as "My teacher!" As if the only reason she was here to teach school was because of him.

"Isn't that the truth?" a small voice inside her head asked irritatingly.

She envisioned his huge smile and the twinkle in his eyes. He was so handsome, with his shiny black hair and his big brown haunting eyes.

She shook her head to clear it, but it was useless. The moonbeams filtered through the soft white muslin curtains on the window, creating shadows on the wall. Why did they all look like Denis McLeod? She turned to face the other direction, hoping to make the images disappear.

At last sleep came and before she knew it the moonbeams had been replaced by the brilliance of the morning sun.

She stretched and climbed out of bed, walking to the window. She gently pulled the curtain back, then gasped as she looked out at the lake. At least he was right about one thing; she had never seen anything as spectacular as the eastern sky with the sun creating bright reds, oranges and purples which reflected not only off the water, but off the bluffs on the sides of the lake as well. The whole horizon looked like it was a blaze of fire. It was pure magic.

"Good morning, Miss Seymour!"

The voice came from directly below her window and across the street. She knew who that voice belonged to before she even looked. How long had he been standing there? Didn't he have anything better to do with his time than to spy on her?

She hurried to draw back from the window and grabbed the quilt from the bed, wrapping it around herself. In spite of what he thought, he didn't own her. He had no right to stare at her in her state of undress, clad only in a sheer voile nightdress.

Something drew her to the window like a magnet. She fought the impulse, but to no avail.

"Hurry," Denis called up to her. "We have a lot of people to meet today."

She wanted to argue with him, to take her own sweet time before she went down, but instead she meekly said, "In a few minutes."

She pulled the curtains shut and went as far to the other side of the room as she could to dress. She donned the same outfit she had worn the night before, sputtering as she did so.

"I've got to find out about using the flat irons," she said. "I'll ask Mrs. Brown."

~*~

"Well, it's about time!" Denis chided as she descended the wide, winding stairway.

"I'll come when I'm good and ready!" she snapped, surprising herself at her own forcefulness.

"Well! Got up on the wrong side of the bed, did we?"

She tried so hard to be angry at him. Why wouldn't he wipe that silly smirk off his face? It would be so much easier if he looked as grouchy as he sounded.

"I certainly did not," she replied, "but you should know! I'll not have you spying on me!"

"Sorry," he said, sounding almost sincere. "I didn't mean..."

"Good morning, Miss Seymour," Thomas Brown interrupted, much to Violet's relief. "Slept well, I trust?"

"Indeed I did," she said. "It was wonderful to have a real bed again. I had nearly forgotten how it felt."

"Then the room is to your liking?" he asked.

"It is perfect," Violet said. "It will be nice and quiet for doing all my teacher stuff." She smiled at Mr. Brown, knowing that he would be able to discern that James had been talking out of school. "That is," she added, "if there isn't too much commotion from the street below."

She glared at Denis as she spoke. If he was smart, he would take the hint and there would be no repeat performances of this morning's episode.

"I'm sure you won't have any problems," Denis said. "You will find that Lake City is a quiet little town, except when the Indians get all riled up."

"Were those...things...out in the street the Indian houses?" she asked, remembering the structures they had passed on their way to the hotel from the lake yesterday. She was so humiliated—wet and all—that she hardly dared look up the whole way, but there were so many it was impossible to miss them.

"Yes," Denis answered. "They are the teepees."

Violet sensed the scorn in Denis's voice. He really did not like the Indians. In fact, it sounded like he hated them. Well, like it or not, she intended to invite the Indian children to attend the school, right along with the white children. If he didn't like it, that was just too bad! It was her school and she'd run it the way she wanted to.

Violet went to the door to inspect her new surroundings. She could see several log houses and three wood frame houses, but dozens of teepees loomed in rows for as far as she could see.

"Were they here first?" she asked Denis.

"Who?"

"The Indians," Violet elaborated. "Or did they come after the other settlers moved in?"

"I'm afraid they were here for years before the white man put in an appearance," Denis explained.

27

"Then we are really living on their land," she said, wondering if the Indians felt like their lives had been invaded.

"No," Denis said, turning his head to spit on the ground in a symbolic action. "The government claimed this land, and the Indian has no right to anything."

"But that's not fair," Violet protested. "Didn't they get anything for it? Surely the government bought it."

"No," Denis said. "Like I said, the Indians have no right to anything. That's as it should be."

Mr. Brown, who was standing nearby, interrupted.

"That's the way it will stay, unless the Indians can force the government into a treaty."

Violet sensed that Mr. Brown was much more sympathetic to the plight of the Indians than Denis was. She couldn't help but wonder why he had such a complete hatred for the Indians. He spoke of them like they were no better than animals.

"Not much chance of that," Denis grumbled. "They're too stubborn."

Violet wondered if he meant the Indians or the government.

"What kind of Indians are they?" she asked.

"The same as all the rest," Denis said. "Savages!"

"Actually," Mr. Brown said, attempting to explain the people who were their neighbors, "they are Sioux. Some people call them Dakotas."

"Either one," Denis said, "it doesn't matter. They don't matter."

"We'll see," Violet said under her breath.

"It's time for a tour of the town," Denis said. "Ready?"

"Not before breakfast," Mr. Brown said, motioning towards the dining room. "Mama has hotcakes and venison sausage ready."

"Sounds wonderful," Violet said enthusiastically, heading towards the door.

"Wonder if she always eats like that," Denis said, shaking his head.

Mr. Brown laughed. "And if she does, how does she keep such a figure?"

Denis looked at the innkeeper in surprise. Granted, he had certainly noticed the new schoolmarm's shape last evening, but he couldn't imagine Mr. Brown paying any attention to such a thing. He wondered if he had told Mrs. Brown his thoughts. No, he decided, Thomas Brown was obviously a very normal man, through and through, but he was not a fool. He would keep such thoughts to himself.

Violet felt a sense of fear as she walked into the dining room and found it empty. She was not ready to be alone with Denis McLeod. She wasn't sure if it was him she didn't trust, or if it was herself she was afraid of. Much to her relief, Mrs. Brown soon came scampering in, her arms laden with heavenly smelling foods.

"Did you sleep well, child?" she asked Violet.

Violet smiled warmly. She was a schoolteacher, not a child, but she supposed that Mrs. Brown considered all the newcomers her children.

"Very well, thank you," Violet said. She looked around the room again. "Where is everyone?" she asked.

Mrs. Brown snickered slightly. "Everyone else has been up for hours. There are chores to be done, work to pursue."

"What time is it?" Violet asked.

Denis took his gold pocket watch out, snapped the cover open and shook his head. "It is nearly nine o'clock, sleepyhead."

Violet blushed in embarrassment. "I don't usually sleep so late," she began to defend herself. "It must be because of the trip. It was very tiring."

"It is quite all right, dear," Mrs. Brown assured her. "I'm sure that once you get the school running you will be up at the first crack of dawn, like the rest of us."

"Yes, I will," Violet said. She looked at Mrs. Brown. "Won't you join us?"

"I'm afraid not," she said. "I have to get things ready for dinner. It is good to have help. Your Aunt Caroline offered first thing this morning."

Violet wondered how many people called Browns' Hotel "home."

"And Uncle King?" she asked, wondering what he was up to. "Where is he?"

"He made arrangements right off to hire Robert White to get started on a house for the family. Alonzo was here bright and early too. With the three of them it won't take too long, but I imagine they feel quite like a trapped bear in such small quarters."

Violet wondered, again, if she would live with them, as she had done before, or if she would remain in the hotel. It would be much more convenient in a real house, and she knew they would never ask her to live anywhere else. After all, they were family. She was one of their own. But it would be much easier to prepare lessons and correct papers without little Henry and Palmer hanging on her constantly.

Not that she didn't love her cousins, but they could be terribly demanding. And now she had a whole town full of children to tend to, not just the two of them.

"What do you plan to show me?" she asked Denis after Mrs. Brown left. She wanted to control the conversation. She didn't know why, but she didn't trust this man. His eyes were such a dark brown they almost seemed black. When he looked at her, it was like he could see beyond her appearance and straight into her soul. She didn't dare think what she felt, lest he should read those thoughts too. No, she must tread carefully.

"I will introduce you to the families who have children," he replied. "They will be most anxious to meet you. They have all had hundreds of questions about you."

"And what did you tell them?" she asked warily.

"About you?" he asked, laughing that deep hearty laugh that was so unpretentious. "What do you think?"

"I—I don't know," Violet said. "I mean, you didn't really know very much about me." She hesitated, then asked, "Did you?"

"Only what Uncle Lath told me," he admitted, "and your Uncle King."

Violet hid her face in her hands. She had no idea what he might have heard, but Uncle King was always a big tease. She hoped he hadn't said anything that would mislead Denis. He was always chiding her for not having a beau; surely he didn't...

"Don't worry," Denis said, trying to sound reassuring. "Everything they said was good."

30

So good, he thought, and they hadn't exaggerated a bit. She was as delightful and intriguing as they told him. And she was certainly as beautiful. Her red hair gave her an impish quality, and her green eyes sparkled like emeralds. He wished he was a little boy again so he could go to school with the other children. Nothing would be more pleasant than to sit and gaze at her hour after hour, day after day.

Violet coughed, bringing him back to reality. "And then what?" she asked.

"Then what?" Denis asked, lost in his own world of fantasy.

"Yes," Violet said, giggling at his lack of attention. "After we meet the children, then what?"

"Oh, yes, your guided tour," Denis said. "Then I will show you the schoolhouse."

"You have an honest-to-goodness schoolhouse?" she asked, her voice filled with excitement. That was more than she had dared to hope for. Back in Morris, Illinois, it was several years before they had been able to move out of the church building. Lake City was a brand new town, yet they already had a schoolhouse. "I am impressed!"

"Well, it's not exactly a schoolhouse yet, but it will be soon. A lot of the men are working on it. Edward Wise donated part of his farmland for it."

Violet began to laugh.

"Did I say something funny?" Denis asked.

"I'm sorry," Violet apologized. "I'm not laughing at you. It is just...it is so funny... Don't you see? The people in Lake City are too good to be true. The hotel is Brown. The builder is White. And the man who gave the land for the school is Wise. It is just so perfect. You are right. I do love Lake City."

Denis tried desperately to stifle his urge to grab her and embrace her. Oh, he knew that was most improper, so he would refrain, but she was so delightful. Her enthusiasm was contagious. Yes, there was no doubt about it; Miss Violet Seymour, schoolmarm extraordinaire, would be the best addition Lake City had known so far.

CHAPTER 4

Violet's eyes opened wide as she stepped outside Browns' Hotel. Earlier, when she had gotten just a glimpse of the town, everything seemed strange. It was her first real view of Lake City. What she saw yesterday, her eyes blinded by water and embarrassment, was almost nonexistent in her memory. She was accustomed to seeing the crude houses people lived in back in Morris, Illinois, but the people in Lake City were obviously both industrious and talented. The homes, whether made of log or planed lumber, bore testimony to the careful planning and artwork that went into each structure. The dominant, overpowering sight, however, was of the many strange triangular teepees of the Indians.

Violet studied them carefully, following Denis down the street. He extended his arm for her, but she defiantly ignored his offer. She did not want people getting the wrong impression of their relationship.

She snickered. Relationship! What relationship? It did not exist. They had just barely met, and here she was imagining that he thought there was more to this mutual interest in the well-being of the children of Lake City than there ought to be.

As they passed several of the teepees, she reached her hand out to feel the taut buffalo hides stretched so that they seemed to be almost transparent. A small funnel of smoke escaped through a hole in the top of each one, indicating that there was a fire burning inside. Some of the hides boasted beautiful colored designs, showing forth the artistic talent of the Indians who dwelled within.

"Don't do that!" Denis insisted, pulling her hand away from the skins.

"Why?" Violet asked. "They are so beautiful; I just wanted to see what they felt like."

Before Denis could explain, a tall, red-skinned man, dressed only in a tight tan buckskin pair of pants, jumped out of the teepee and began shouting something at them which she did not understand at all.

Violet froze. Maybe Denis was right. All she could see of this man who loomed like a giant in front of her was his extremely muscular framework and the tomahawk he held in his hand, poised as if ready for action.

"I am sorry," Violet said, certain that he would not understand her any more than she did him. "I was just admiring your handiwork."

She hoped that her voice would soothe the savage beast. She certainly meant no harm.

A younger man, probably in his late teens, Violet guessed, stepped out beside them. He spoke to the older man, then turned his attention to Violet.

"I told him you were all right," he explained to Violet. "He says he is sorry he spoke so rudely to you. It is just that we have had so many illnesses since the white man has come that he does not trust any of them."

"What kind of illnesses?" Violet asked.

"We do not know," the young man replied. "We only know that many of our people have died. Just this morning the spirits of Rattling Leaf and Little Flower left us."

"I am sorry," Violet said, extending her hand to his in a sympathetic gesture. "Is there anything I can do?"

"There is nothing you can do except leave us alone."

"Isn't there a physician in Lake City?" she asked, turning to Denis, who was trying frantically to pull her away.

"My father," the Indian lad explained, "is our medicine man. The spirits are not pleased by the white man's presence. They do not heed my father anymore. It is because of Wenona that their spirits have left us."

"But how?" Violet asked. "And who is Wenona?"

"Wenona is the chief's granddaughter," Denis explained.

"She is a mere child?" Violet asked.

"She has seen only six snows," the young Indian lad said.

"How did she cause these deaths?" Violet asked, trying her best to understand.

"She has played with the white children," the Indian boy explained.

"That makes no sense at all," Violet said.

"It makes all the sense," the boy continued. "The white man brought much bad sickness. Our people cannot fight them."

"What is he talking about?" Violet asked Denis.

"I will explain it later," Denis said, taking Violet by the arm, urging her to leave.

"I do not know what I can do to help," Violet said, "but perhaps if your children are educated it might someday help. I am the new schoolteacher. I do hope you will help me spread the word that soon there will be a real school for all the children of Lake City."

The medicine man spoke to his son, and his son answered, pointing to Violet as he spoke.

"What are they saying?" she asked Denis.

"The old man says he will not allow his children to attend the school. Now, will you please come with me? We have to get out of here."

He did not waste any time, but pulled hard on her hand. Frightened, yet fascinated by this encounter, she went with him. Denis led her in the direction of a small log house and pushed her inside.

"Whose home is this?" Violet asked, not wanting to intrude on some poor unprepared person.

"Mine," Denis replied. "Mine and Uncle Lath's."

"And where is Uncle Lath?" Violet asked, looking around for someone to protect her.

"Out on the ferry, of course," Denis said.

"And why aren't you out there helping him? I thought you said the two of you had a partnership."

"We do," Denis said, "but he said I could spend the day getting you acquainted with everyone."

Violet wanted to run away. Why did being alone with him make her so terribly, horribly uncomfortable? He had been a perfect gentleman, still...

She headed for the door, but Denis positioned himself directly in front of her, blocking her escape.

"I think we'd better have a talk before you take out on your own. There," he said, pointing to a small wooden settle in front of the roughhewn stone fireplace. "Go sit down!"

Violet went obediently. She felt suddenly like a little girl, being ordered to do something by Uncle King.

"That's better," Denis said, smiling that devilish grin at her. "This is all new to you, so I won't fault you for the errors you have made."

"Errors?" Violet snapped at him. "What errors? I was just talking to one of the men in town! I did nothing wrong."

"That's your first mistake," Denis said, "thinking you can do no wrong. For your own safety you had better listen, and listen good."

"I'm not taking orders from you," Violet argued. "You don't own me."

"Oh, but I do," Denis said. "Did you forget that it was me who asked you to come here to teach our children? If I hadn't written that stupid letter to your Uncle King you would still be back in Illinois. Maybe that would be better for everybody concerned. Don't you see? The white man and the Indians—the savages—they must be kept apart. You can't trust them, Violet. They are as sly as the foxes they hunt. You cannot expect them to send their children to our schools. Their ways are different from ours. Besides, you heard Healing Waters say himself that he would not allow their children to attend our schools. They don't want to be with us any more than we want to be with them."

"I heard his son tell me that, but he could have said anything. How is it that you, if you hate them so much, can understand their language?"

"A man does what he has to in order to survive."

"And your communicating with the Indians helps you survive?" she asked.

"Someone has to defend our rights to them," Denis explained.

"And you were chosen?"

"Strange as it may seem," he said, "I was chosen."

"But why?" Violet asked, not understanding any of this unusual arrangement. If they wanted someone to interact with the Indians why on earth would they select the one person who probably trusted them the least?

"Of course," Denis said. "Don't you see? It makes perfect sense. I know they can't be trusted. That makes me more reliable than someone who might slant things in favor of the beasts. Besides, other than Reverend Hazlett and Doc Vilas, I have more education than anyone else in town. Guess a good learnin' counts for something, even in these parts."

"Remember to act like it," Violet teased.

"Tell me about Wenona," she said, anxious to change the subject. "Why is it her fault that Rattling Leaf and Little Flower died?"

"There is a family just outside of Lake City—the Bergans. They are Germans. Three of their children got smallpox and died." He paused a few moments before continuing. "Wenona had become friends with one of their girls. When she heard that they had died, she felt really bad so she went out to see them. She took Little Flower with her so they could talk to each other."

"Little Flower speaks English?" Violet asked.

"A few words," Denis said, "but children can communicate sometimes without words. They seemed almost like sisters when you would see them together. So different—yet so alike."

"But why should that make the chief so angry?"

"That wasn't the end of it," Denis said. "Mrs. Bergan gave Little Flower a blanket from each of their children. Wenona was so proud of those blankets. She kept one and she gave one of them to Little Flower, her sister, and the other one to Rattling Leaf. Before long, the two children were ill with the fever too. The chief blamed it on Wenona and the blankets. He said the blankets brought the bad spirits that killed their children to the Indian camp. He said it was the white man's way of killing their people." Denis hid his face in his hands to try to hide his tears from Violet.

Violet was shocked by Denis's reaction. He really does have a heart after all, she thought.

When he regained his composure he said, "Truth is, Black Cloud—the chief—was probably right. The smallpox spreads like a wildfire after lightening hits a dry forest."

"What will the chief do to Wenona?"

"I'm not certain," Denis admitted, "but I have a feeling it won't be pleasant. There is nothing you can do about it. Promise me that you won't interfere. It could be dangerous, for both you and Wenona. I have a stake in your survival, you know."

He reached over and took hold of Violet's hand. She jerked it away quickly.

"Denis McLeod, don't you go trying to sweet talk me! I'm not dumb either. I won't fall for some silly prattle about how educated you are. Why, look here!" She grabbed a letter which was lying on the small table beside the settle where she was sitting. "You think you are so smart. Not likely! You can't even spell your own name right. Everybody knows you always spell Denis with two n's."

Denis glared at her for a few moments, then broke into that infuriating loud laughter he was so good at. Violet winced. She didn't see anything amusing in the situation at all. He was just laughing to taunt her. Oh, he was the most exasperating person she had ever had the misfortune of meeting. She rose to her feet and started to leave.

"Where do you think you are going?" he asked.

"It doesn't matter," she said. "I can manage on my own, thank you kindly. You have done quite enough for one day. I will make my own acquaintance with the people of the village. There are not so many of them that I can't find them by myself."

"And you think they will just open their doors to you, a stranger?" Denis asked.

"Yes," Violet insisted, "I do. They must all know that a new schoolteacher is here. You said yourself that you told them all about me."

"Knowing about you is one thing. Accepting you is quite another."

"I do believe that I can present myself in such a way," Violet said, "that they will not only open their doors to me, but their hearts as well. Nothing is more precious to a family than their children. It is the well-being and future of those children that I am here to nurture."

She pulled herself up to her full five-foot-two stature, the fire dancing in her bright green eyes and her face as red as the hair on her head. "Good day, Mr. McLeod."

She walked across the wood-plank floor, her heels clicking loudly, and reached for the door. It was stuck, so she pushed harder.

"What's the matter with the door?" a man asked from outside.

Violet jumped back, unprepared for a visitor. He hadn't knocked, but apparently felt secure in entering unannounced.

As she removed her hand from the door the man's force caused the door to open with unexpected ease, sending him into the house like an attacking animal. He looked up at Violet, a grin on his face, and extended his hand to her.

"I didn't know you were entertaining a young lady," he said. "You are the new schoolmarm, I assume?"

"Violet Seymour," she said, accepting his offer of a handshake from his position on the floor, where he sat with his legs sprawled out in front of him. "Yes, I am the new schoolteacher. And you, I presume, must be Uncle Lath."

"The very same," he said, his voice thick with a Scottish brogue. "Lathrop McLeod, at your service, ma'am. It's a pleasure to have you here in Lake City. A true pleasure, indeed."

"What are you doing home?" Denis asked his uncle.

"Nobody's going any place today," Uncle Lath answered. "I s'pose you heard about Rattling Leaf and Little Flower."

"Healing Waters told us," Denis said.

Uncle Lath's face waned. "You talked to Healing Waters?"

Violet recognized the shock that registered in his voice. Had she really done something wrong? Denis said she had committed some "error." Maybe he was right. She would have to learn more about life in Lake City before she did something that might cause some terrible harm to someone.

"Yes," Denis said, looking accusingly at Violet. "It was her fault."

"I didn't know..." Violet said. "No one told me..."

"Well, next time I hope you'll know better," Uncle Lath warned. "Anyway, what's done is done. But with the death of Rattling Leaf and Little Flower—well, it's got everybody spooked."

"Spooked?" Violet asked. Surely they couldn't believe in the superstitions of the Indians. The spirits couldn't be floating around somewhere, waiting to invade them with some evil.

"Yes, spooked," Uncle Lath said. "I can't explain it, but when I was out on the lake I swear you could feel something strange lurking out there. I looked around, but I couldn't see anything. Nothing at all."

"I'll take the little boat out," Denis said. "Maybe I can spot something. My eyes are better than yours."

"I don't think..." Uncle Lath said, afraid of what his nephew might encounter.

"I'll go along," Violet said, intrigued by the mysterious attitude of these seemingly sane, rational people.

"Not on your life!" Uncle Lath said.

"No way!" Denis echoed. "No woman has ever gone to hunt for the spirits, and they'll not start now."

"And if you find the spirits?" Violet teased. "What will you do with them?"

"Bring them back to you," Denis threatened. "Then see what you can do with them. You think you can educate them?"

Denis disappeared in a flash.

"I'll walk you back to the hotel," Uncle Lath offered.

As they made their way along the one street in town, he pointed to a group of people nearby.

"It's Uncle King!" she exclaimed. "Is that where he is building his house?"

"Yes," Uncle Lath said. "He has to build in this end of town."

"He has to?" Violet asked, puzzled. "But why?"

"Because of Caroline," he explained. "Caroline and the Keiths."

"I don't understand," Violet admitted.

"This end of town, where Denis and I live, has been declared Little Scotland. Since King married Caroline, and she is a Keith— and a Scot—they have no choice in where they live."

"Is that bad?" Violet asked innocently.

"Ach!" Uncle Lath remarked, laughing heartily, the same way Denis laughed. "Only if you are not a Scotsman yourself! Then it is ter-r-r-r-rible! But if you are blessed enough to be a Scotsman through and through, then you are truly one of the lucky ones."

CHAPTER 5

Violet's eyes seemed glued to the lake, watching Denis in his rowboat. He got smaller and smaller as he moved out towards the center of the lake.

Lath McLeod escorted Violet back towards the hotel. He spoke very little. He was right; there was something eerie filling the air.

Suddenly from one of the teepees came a loud, mournful wail. "Me choonk she! Me choonk she!" It was repeated, over and over again, filling the still air with its message.

Violet grabbed hold of Lath's arm.

"What is that?" she asked.

He placed his hand reassuringly on top of hers. "That is Little Flower's mother, Rose Petal. It is her way of dealing with her daughter's death. Don't let it frighten you. It simply means My child. It is customary for the mother to wail in this manner."

As they walked, the chant continued until the strange words, Me choonk she, were indelibly etched in Violet's mind. She knew she would never forget them. Her heart ached for the mother. She might be different from the white people, but surely her loss was felt as deeply as that of any mother.

"Why does Denis hate the Indians so much?" she asked.

"Who said he did?"

"Nobody," Violet said. "They didn't have to. I could tell from what he did say, even though he didn't put it into words, how he feels about them."

"Maybe some day he will tell you," Lath said. He knew the reasons so well, but it was not his place to explain his nephew's actions. "I would be very careful about asking him," he warned.

"Do you hate them too?" Violet asked.

"No," Lath replied. "I have tried to, but I can't. They seem so—human."

Violet breathed a sigh of relief. If Lath McLeod could accept the Indians the way they were, then she felt more comfortable with her own quest to include them in the school, despite Denis's objections.

The sound of the woman had caused her to take her eyes from the lake. When she turned back to look for Denis she became nearly hysterical.

"He's gone! Something terrible has happened! I know it has!"

Lath looked out over the calm waters, but he did not see Denis either.

"You cannot see such a small vessel all the way across," he explained. "He is well experienced on the water. He has just gotten beyond our vision. With it so still today there is no need to worry."

Violet tugged at Lath's sleeve, then pointed in a totally different direction than Denis had headed when he left.

"Look! Over there! Isn't that Denis? No one else was on the lake."

Lath squinted, trying to make out the figure to be sure that it was indeed Denis.

"Yes, it appears to be," he said finally. "He is headed for Maiden Rock. Whatever can he be doing?"

"Maiden Rock?" Violet asked, recognizing the name. "That's where Uncle Alonzo lives."

"Well, not exactly," Lath explained. "Alonzo lives in the town of Maiden Rock. Denis appears to be headed for the rock itself."

"The rock?" Violet asked.

"Yes," Lath said, opening the door to Browns' Hotel for Violet. "Come in and sit down. I'll tell you the tale of Maiden Rock."

They went to the divan and sat down. Mr. Brown greeted them with a friendly smile.

"There was a young Indian maiden, a Dakota, who fell in love with a Chippewa brave."

Violet listened intently as Lath continued to spin the tale.

"Her father would not allow them to marry. The Dakota and Chippewa have always been enemies. The Chippewa brave went away, rejected by the woman he loved. He never knew that she was willing to desert her own people to follow him. When she learned that he was gone she plunged from the rock to her death."

Violet sat, staring at her hands. "That is so sad," was all she could manage to say above the lump in her throat. She wondered if anyone really loved another person that deeply. Would she ever find such devotion to anyone? Certainly it could not be to Denis McLeod.

She shook her head, surprised at the turn her thoughts had just taken. She had no right to think such things. She was here at Denis McLeod's request, but for nothing more than to run the school. Nothing more!

When she was able to speak again she asked Lath, "What was the maiden's name?"

"Wenona," he answered.

"That is a strange name," Violet said, "and the same name as the chief's granddaughter."

"Wenona simply indicated that she was the oldest daughter. Every Dakota in that position is called Wenona until she earns her own name."

"And how does she earn her name?" Violet asked, completely entranced by the strange customs of the Dakota people.

"When she becomes old enough for something she has done to determine what her post in life is, then she is given an appropriate name."

"Like Rose Petal?" Violet asked. "Healing Waters' wife?"

"Yes, exactly like that," Lath said. "I have heard the story of Rose Petal's name. Healing Waters was administering the medicine dance for the chief's son. The chief's daughter offered him a potion she had made from the petals of the wild rose. Healing Waters accepted it graciously. He covered the young brave's forehead with them, and he was cured almost immediately."

"And that is how the girl became Rose Petal?" Violet asked.

Lath nodded. Suddenly there was a loud commotion outside. They ran to the door to see what it was all about. A large group of Indians had assembled and were dancing in a circle around two large boxes.

"What is that?" Violet asked, clinging tightly to Lath's arm.

"It is the coffins for Rattling Leaf and Little Flower," he explained.

"But they are so big!" Violet exclaimed. She had seen more than her share of coffins in her lifetime, but none as large as these. "Why?"

"The Indians wrap the bodies of the departed in layers and layers of cloth and blankets. By the time they are finished, they need a large coffin. It is a good thing that they are important people. I told you that Little Flower is the chief's granddaughter. Sometimes they take the bodies and hang them up in the woods before they bury them. Because it is Black Cloud's granddaughter and her friend, they believe their spirits have already departed for a better place. They have not been wrapped yet. That will happen tonight. They are on display for the people to say their farewells and to pray for their spirits' journey."

Rose Petal made her way to the box that contained the tiny body of Little Flower, her daughter, her flesh and blood. The tears flowed freely as she approached the box. She knelt beside the box and wailed, banging her hands against the box, creating an almost melodic sound, like it was a drum.

Violet and Uncle Lath watched from afar, not daring to intrude on the spiritual sense of the Indian gathering. When the drumming ceased, the silence was almost deafening by contrast. Rose Petal, still kneeling on the ground, reached into the box and tenderly ran her hands over Little Flower's body, slowly, deliberately, as if she was trying to memorize each little detail, saving it forever in her mind—and in her heart.

As Rose Petal's hands passed over Little Flower, she slowly and silently unfastened the beaded necklace from her daughter's neck. She palmed it, hiding it from view of those who stood beyond her. Finally, she got to her feet, bent over and kissed Little Flower on the forehead, and walked away, going into her teepee, the tears still streaming down her face, to be alone with her grief.

Rose Petal looked around for Wenona, but there was no sign of her. She tenderly tucked Little Flower's necklace into the pouch that was tied around her waist by a leather thong.

She pondered Wenona's absence and once again began to weep and to wail. From outside the teepee, the group left her alone, not knowing that she was mourning the loss—not of one daughter, but of two daughters. They did not know that Black Cloud had ordered Wenona not to darken the doors of any member of the tribe. He blamed her, and her alone, for the death of Rattling Leaf and Little Flower because of bringing the evil spirits in on the blankets.

When Rose Petal asked Black Cloud why Wenona had not gotten ill as well as the other two, he explained it away easily.

"Because she has befriended the white man their witchcraft has protected her. Their spirits are dangerous to our spirits. They battle here, and in the worlds beyond. Wenona must not remain here with us."

~*~

Rose Petal wondered what Black Cloud had done with Wenona, where he had taken her. She knew he would not physically harm her, but banishing her would be extremely dangerous. She said a silent prayer to the grandfathers for her daughter's protection.

~*~

Violet scanned the children who stood on the sidelines of the dance.

"Where is Wenona?" she asked Uncle Lath.

Lath looked them over carefully.

"She is not here," he said. "That is strange."

"The poor child is probably frightened to death. She is probably tucked away in their teepee, afraid to come out."

~*~

Denis held one oar down in the water and turned the boat with the other one, almost as if he was forced to act against his will. Uncle Lath was definitely right; there was something very strange about the lake today. Before he realized it, he was headed straight for the high craggy slopes of Maiden Rock. As he neared it, an unknown force caused him to stop and listen carefully.

It was silent. Such dead silence—the spirits seemed to scream through the stillness. He sat, not moving a muscle, as if the very air was enchanted.

Then, through the quiet came a sharp bleating sound. It was pleading for help, although it certainly did not resemble any human voice he had ever heard. It stopped, as quickly as it had begun. A few moments of the silence again, then the wail of the wounded animal once more crept through the air.

Denis headed the boat directly for the rock. When he neared it he tossed his anchor overboard and jumped out, wading—shiny black leather boots and all—for the edge of the rock. Carefully, slowly, he made his way up the steep precipice. His foot, set on the tiny ledges, slipped and he scraped his hands as he grabbed at the rocks to save him. Once again, even more slowly, he wound his way up the rocks towards the cries of the injured creature.

When the shrieks stopped he would stay still until they began again. He didn't want to end up in the wrong place, nor did he want to frighten the animal, whatever it was. He wondered if it had been captured by a vulture and deposited atop the rocks when the bird spotted a more appetizing, appealing victim. It was hard to imagine how or why something would mount the rock to its peak of its own free will.

He could tell he was almost at the spot where the animal was. He had to move carefully so he didn't frighten it. If he did, one wrong move could send the poor thing hurling through space like the Indian maiden of old.

When he was finally high enough to see what was making the noise, he nearly lost his footing. He never expected to find a small child there, huddled just at the edge of a crevice between the rocks.

"What are you doing here?" he asked.

When she did not answer, Denis repeated the question in her own language. He recognized her, even though he had never spoken to her before. He knew he would have to approach her slowly, carefully, so as to not frighten her. He had seen her with the Bergan children many times.

"Go away," the little girl answered, sliding in her squatting position ever closer to the crack in the rocks when she saw him.

"Don't move!" Denis ordered. "I am here to help you."

"I told you, 'Go away!' I don't want your help. I don't want anyone's help. I just want to stay here and die."

"Whatever it is that's troubling you," Denis said, speaking slowly and distinctly—not for her benefit, but so he would not make any mistakes in the language which was so foreign to him—"it can't be that bad."

"You don't know," the girl challenged, then began to wail that high shrill chant again.

"Then why don't you tell me?" he asked, trying to make her relax so he could grab her and take her to the safety of his boat below.

"You don't know," she said. "You could never understand."

"Why don't you tell me, and we'll see," Denis said.

She sat in silence for what seemed like ages to Denis. He just waited patiently until at last she began to talk.

"Black Cloud says they are gone. Their spirits soared like the eagles to other places."

The tiny girl began to sob loudly. Denis extended his hand towards her, carefully, so he wouldn't frighten her.

"Rattling Leaf and Little Flower, they are your family?" Denis asked in her native tongue, trying to find a common ground to talk to her.

"Yes," she said, wiping her tears on the back of her hand. "Did you know them?"

"A little," Denis said. He felt a shiver run up and down his spine. By all rights, he should feel the same hatred for this child that he felt for all the other Indians. Instead, he felt a strange sympathy.

"You can't know how it feels," she said. "I asked Black Cloud how long they would be gone, and he said they are never coming back."

"That's right," Denis said, wishing he could find some words to console her, but there were none. How well he knew that nothing anyone said could make any difference. "Once they are gone, they are gone forever."

"How long is forever?" the child asked him.

Denis looked at her, his eyes filled with compassion.

"It is longer than either you or I can imagine," he said. "It is longer than all the snows that Iron Walker has passed."

The girl smiled through her tears. Everyone knew that Iron Walker was the oldest Dakota living. Although no one knew exactly how old he was, most people figured him to be well over one hundred years old.

"You know Iron Walker?"

"Everyone knows Iron Walker," Denis said, pleased to see her smile. "He has lived many snows. How many snows have you passed?"

"Five," she said, holding up all of the fingers on one hand. "This many. How many snows are you?"

Denis laughed. "Too many," he said. "I do not have enough fingers."

The girl laughed at him. With no warning, she scurried over beside him. He gently placed his arm around her, drawing her close. He felt himself going back over the years to when he was just two or three years older than she was. His own eyes filled with tears.

"Don't cry," she said, putting her arms around his neck. "It is not bad to be many snows old."

"I am not crying because I am old," Denis assured her. "It is just, I am so sorry about your sister and Rattling Leaf."

"Me too," she said, still clinging to him. She studied his face carefully, then asked, "Why are you sad?"

"Because," Denis explained, "many snows ago, when I was not much older than you are now, my mother and father went away too, like Little Flower and Rattling Leaf."

"And you missed them?" she asked.

"Very much," Denis said. "Every day when I woke up I expected my mother to come get me up, but she never came again."

The two strangers, so different, yet sharing a common bond, sat together for some time. They did not speak. It was not necessary. They understood each other completely in the midst of their silence.

Finally, Denis spoke. "Come with me to my boat. I will take you back to Black Cloud."

"No!" she shouted. "I will not go back to him! I will stay here instead."

"But why don't you want to go to Black Cloud?" Denis asked, surprised by her reaction. "He is your grandfather."

"He ordered me to stay away," she confessed shyly.

"Very well," Denis said. "There is a new lady in town. She arrived just yesterday. She is a very nice lady. She would like you. She likes all children. She is going to teach all the children in Lake City. I will take you to her. She will care for you."

The girl hesitated. "But she is a white woman?"

"Yes," Denis said, "but she likes the Dakota children. Just this morning she asked Healing Waters to let the Dakota children go to her school."

"She would like me?" she asked, smiling again, "even if I am Dakota?"

"She would love you," Denis said, sure that he spoke the truth, "but before I take you to her, maybe you should tell me your name." He was certain she was still known as Wenona, but he felt that she would not expect him to know that.

"It is Wenona," she said slowly, "like the maiden of the rock."

"But you will not become like the maiden of the rock," Denis said, running his hands across her sleek black hair. "You will have people to love you."

Denis gathered her into his arms and began the steep descent into the boat.

"What are you called?" she asked Denis.

"Denis," he replied simply.

She looked up at him, her big black eyes glistening. "I will call you Arms-of-Steel," she said. "I like it better."

"And I will call you Gentle Lamb," he said, knowing that sooner or later she would outgrow her common title of Wenona. "Today you earned your own name."

49

CHAPTER 6

Violet paced back and forth in the hotel lobby. She would not rest until Denis returned. Lath tried to assure her that with the water so still nothing could harm him out on the lake, but Violet sensed that he was convinced that there was more than an ill wind blowing in the air today. He stayed with her, going to the door to look out from time to time.

"Here he comes!" he finally shouted. "He is carrying something."

Violet ran out into the street to meet him. She couldn't wait one second longer; she had already waited far too long. Shock filled her when she realized that it was an Indian child in his arms.

"Who is that?" she asked. "And why is she with you? Is she hurt?"

"Not physically," Denis answered. "Violet—Miss Seymour—I would like you to meet Gentle Lamb. She is Black Cloud's granddaughter and Rose Petal's daughter."

He set her down on the ground. She stretched her chubby little brown hand out towards Violet, just like Denis had shown her on their way back to shore. He was right; she did want to make a good impression on the new lady, especially if she was going to take care of her.

"I am very pleased to meet you, Gentle Lamb," Violet said, smiling warmly at the child.

"Does she speak English?" Violet asked Denis.

"Not yet," he said, then added, "well, a few words."

"What do you mean?" Violet inquired.

"I think you had better come over here and sit down," Denis said, taking her by the hand and leading her to the divan. "Keep an eye on her, will you, Uncle Lath?"

"Sure," Lath replied. "Come on, Gentle Lamb. Let's go get you something to eat. You look hungry."

Even though she didn't understand, she followed him willingly.

"The poor little thing," Violet said when she and Denis were alone. "She must be scared to death after everything that has happened to her family."

"She was," Denis said. "I found her hiding up at the peak of Maiden Rock."

"How awful!" Violet exclaimed. "How did you know?"

"I heard a loud wailing sound from up there. I thought it was an animal trapped, so I went to rescue it."

"And it was Gentle Lamb?" Violet asked. "I guess she would seem like an animal, all frightened like that."

"Yes, that is why I gave her that name. Before that, she was Wenona, the one I told you about."

Violet looked at him in surprise. She knew how he felt about the Indians, but there was nothing but kindness reflected in his eyes now.

"You named her?" she asked.

"Yes, and she named me." He shrugged his shoulders and laughed. "I guess I finally grew up today."

Violet laughed with him. "I'd say it's about time," she teased. "So what kind of a name did Gentle Lamb decide you deserved?"

He smiled at her, his deep dimples slightly red. "Arms-of-Steel," he said.

Violet's mind went back to just one short day ago. It seemed like an eternity had passed since that dreadful moment when she had gone overboard. But she had to admit, "Arms-of-Steel" suited him well. Yes, she had felt those same arms carry her to safety, just as they had no doubt done with Gentle Lamb.

"Well, do you like it?" he asked, still grinning at her.

"It fits you very well," she said, not elaborating any more on the subject. "What did you want to talk to me about?"

"You read minds as well as books?" he asked.

"You said I had better sit down. It was obvious you had something in mind."

At least it isn't something unsightly or off-color, she thought, or you would have taken me somewhere besides the lobby of the only hotel in town. "Violet!" she scolded herself silently. "Quit that!"

"Okay, here's the plan," he said, looking at her seriously. She waited for him to continue. "I told Gentle Lamb that I would take her home to Black Cloud. He's her grandfather."

"Lath told me he's the chief," Violet interrupted.

"That's right," Denis agreed. "But Gentle Lamb, she said he blamed her for the deaths. He has cast her out."

"She can't live on her own!" Violet insisted. "She's just a little girl."

"Only five snows old," Denis said, holding his five fingers up, exactly as Gentle Lamb had done.

Violet smiled warmly at him. She thought of his earlier reaction to the Indians, and she knew it was a great sacrifice for him to offer help to the child.

"But how can you and Lath—two bachelors—take care of a little girl like Gentle Lamb? You wouldn't have any idea what to do with her."

"You're quite right," Denis said. "I knew you would understand."

"Understand what?"

"Why she would have to live with you. You must take care of her."

Violet's mouth dropped open. She had helped Aunt Caroline and Uncle King with Henry and Palmer, so she knew how to tend children, but having one you were completely responsible for, that was quite a different matter.

"But what if Black Cloud decides he wants her back with him?" she asked.

"Then we will have to fight Black Cloud."

"You want me to fight the chief of the tribe?" she asked in disbelief. "I could never..."

"I didn't say you," Denis said. "I said we."

"I didn't know there was a we," Violet argued.

"Maybe there wasn't, but there is now. For Gentle Lamb's sake, there has to be a we."

"But I don't know their language at all. I wouldn't even be able to understand anything she said."

"She is a smart little tyke," Denis said. "She will learn English easily. Besides, I will help you learn some Sioux. It will be good for you."

"I don't know," Violet said, shaking her head and trying to formulate other arguments in her mind.

"You want her to go with someone who might mistreat her? God only knows what Black Cloud might do to her if she tried to go back. Could you live with yourself, knowing you could have protected her?"

"No," Violet answered slowly. This wasn't fair! He was using dirty fighting tactics. He shouldn't be laying guilt at her feet. After all, he rescued her. She had no part of it.

"You wanted a way to reach the Indian children for the school," Denis argued. "You told Healing Waters so yourself, just this morning."

"But don't you see? They will think I have kidnapped the child, that I have turned her against her own people. That will only make them trust me less, not more."

"We will cross that bridge when we come to it," Denis said. "For the time being, let's go join Uncle Lath and Gentle Lamb." He looked at her, his eyes pleading. "Will you keep her? At least for now? She has already had enough of a loss for the present."

"On one condition," Violet said, looking him square in those big dark brown eyes.

"Which is?" he asked.

"That you tell me what changed your mind?"

"About what?"

"About her. About Indians," Violet said simply.

"She can't help what she is," he said, trying to explain without committing himself. "She is just a poor, helpless child. At her age there is no difference in the color of the skin." He did not tell Violet that Gentle Lamb had been hesitant about staying with the new lady in town because she was white.

"There is more to it than that," Violet insisted.

"Someday I will tell you, but not today. I can't today."

Violet felt a closeness to Denis McLeod she had not known before, not even when he had his arms around her and was dragging her to shore. Something told her that they shared a lot more than an interest in the education of the children of Lake City, Minnesota. Some day she would know, she vowed, but he was right. Today was not the day.

CHAPTER 7

Gentle Lamb came running to Denis when she saw him and Violet come into the dining room at the hotel. Violet stood by as they exchanged excited chatter which meant nothing at all to her. Denis took her by the hand and led her back to the table, where the three of them joined Lath.

"What did she say?" Violet asked anxiously.

"She asked if you liked her," Denis explained.

Violet smiled warmly at the little girl. She reached out and touched her cheek tenderly. "I like you very much," she said, hoping her face and eyes would relay her message when words failed. The smile that brightened Gentle Lamb's face assured her that it did exactly that.

"She says she likes you too," Denis said, interpreting for Gentle Lamb.

"Tell her I will be very happy to have her live with me. My bed is big enough for both of us."

Denis began to give the message to Gentle Lamb, then laughed as he stopped. "I don't know the word for bed," he said. "The Dakota have no beds. They sleep on hides or mats on the floor." His face lit up with an idea. He spoke again to Gentle Lamb. The look on her face was one of eagerness and anticipation.

"What did you tell her now?" Violet asked.

"I told her that she would be sleeping on a very big pillow. They all have a feather pillow; a featherbed is just like it, only much bigger. She said she will sleep like she is on a cloud."

"We will have a good time," Violet said enthusiastically.

"No regrets?" Denis asked.

"How could I?" Violet asked. "She is adorable."

"I knew you would like her," Denis said, relief registering in his voice.

"She has to be the closest thing to an angel," Violet said, winking at Denis. "It takes a miracle to capture your heart."

"Not as much as you might think," he said, leaving her to draw her own conclusions.

Denis said something, then handed her a small packet of paper he took out of his jacket pocket.

"I told her that if she needs to tell you something she can draw you a picture of what she is trying to say. You do have a pen and some ink, don't you?"

"Yes," Violet said, trying to sound hurt. "What kind of a teacher do you think I am?"

After they all finished eating, Violet took Gentle Lamb and led her up the stairs to her room at the end of the corridor. When they were inside, Gentle Lamb went to the window and pulled the curtain back. She stared out for a long time, not talking, not moving. Finally, Violet heard the tiny sobs that were escaping from her broken heart.

Gentle Lamb pointed to one of the teepees and said something. Violet knew, instinctively, that she was indicating the house of her parents. She went to the girl and placed her arm around her shoulder, drawing her to herself for comfort. The gentle whimperings exploded into loud sobs.

Violet ached for the poor little girl. She thought of her own parents, who had died when Violet was too young to even remember them. Which was worse? she wondered. How she wished she had known Rattling Leaf and Little Flower so she could tell Gentle Lamb about them when she was older. Or was she old enough to bear their imprint on her mind forever?

When she had cried herself out, Gentle Lamb went to the bed and sat on it, bouncing up and down. Slowly, cautiously, a smile crept across her face. She repeated a word over and over again. Remembering Denis's explanation of the bed as a "big pillow,"

Violet took the pillow and showed it to Gentle Lamb, repeating the word "pillow" several times. Slowly, but distinctly, she soon formed the word "pillow," much to her delight. Gentle Lamb said the Sioux word for "pillow." Violet followed suit, repeating the strange-sounding word, and Gentle Lamb jumped up and down even more excitedly than before. "Bed," Violet said, patting the bed with her hand. Gentle Lamb said something which Violet assumed was "big pillow," since that was how Denis had described it to her.

After a while of their talking, exchanging words and then phrases, Violet went to the ewer and basin to wash in preparation for retiring for the night. Gentle Lamb studied her actions with interest and curiosity. When Violet was done, she motioned for Gentle Lamb to follow suit.

Gentle Lamb shook her head, protesting. Finally Violet gave her a pen and some ink, and she drew a picture of the river. Then she placed a tiny figure in the river. Violet understood; she had never bathed anywhere except in the river.

Violet took the pen from her and drew a sun just beginning to rise on the edge of the river. Yes, in the morning she would take Gentle Lamb to the river to bathe.

~*~

In the morning Violet awoke with the first rays of the sun. She turned to face Gentle Lamb, trying to decide if the whole last two days had been a dream or if they had really happened. Seeing the child, still sound asleep, she knew it was real.

She got up quietly, trying not to disturb Gentle Lamb, and went to the window. She carefully pulled a thick robe on first. She looked up and down the street, but Denis was nowhere in sight. She didn't know whether to be relieved or disappointed.

She dressed, selecting a brown calico skirt and a light yellow blouse. She ran her hands over it, not really satisfied that it was in its best shape, but determined more than ever to ask Mrs. Brown about using her flatirons.

In spite of Violet's efforts to be quiet, Gentle Lamb soon stirred, raised herself up on one elbow and looked at her. Shortly, a smile appeared, reassuring Violet that she had made the right choice—the only choice.

Gentle Lamb jumped out of bed and dressed in a hurry. Violet had given her one of her blouses to sleep in, and the smooth cotton material felt foreign to her. As she tugged at the little suede dress her mother had made for her from deer hide, she felt the comfort of it against her skin. She smiled, remembering how she had watched her mother stitch it with a porcupine needle.

"It is pretty," Violet said, running her hands over the garment. "Pretty," she repeated. Then she drew a picture of a flower and a sunset over the lake. "Pretty," she said.

Gentle Lamb grasped the new word quickly. She took her tiny hand and felt Violet's thick red curls. "Pretty," she said.

Violet took her by the hand and headed towards the door. "Maybe Denis is waiting for us," she suggested.

Questions filled Gentle Lamb's eyes. Violet reached for a piece of the paper and drew a picture of a man wearing Denis's captain's hat. "Denis," she said, pointing to the figure.

"Denis," Gentle Lamb repeated.

They made their way together to the hotel lobby, only to find both Denis and Lath waiting for them. Gentle Lamb ran to him excitedly. "Denis!" she shouted. "Denis!"

Denis's face glowed at the way she pronounced his name. She had never called him anything before, except the Sioux word for Arms-of-Steel.

"Good morning, Gentle Lamb," he said, picking her up in his arms and swinging her around. In Sioux he asked her if she slept well.

"Bed," she said, nodding at the memory of the soft fluffy space she had occupied during the night.

"Yes, it was a fine bed," Denis said. He turned to Violet. "I told you she was smart."

"And you were right. She learned quite a few words last night and this morning."

"And you?" Denis asked.

"Yes," Violet admitted, "I learned some too."

He grinned at Gentle Lamb and said something to her. She giggled delightedly, pointing to Violet and nodding her head in agreement with whatever Denis had said.

"This isn't fair!" Violet protested. "What did you tell her?"

He said a few words to Gentle Lamb, and she nodded again.

"She says I can tell you," Denis said, teasing her by a long pause. "I asked her if you learned any of her words. She said 'Yes, she did. She can say bed and pillow.' She said I was right; you are smart too."

Violet reached out and playfully struck Denis on the arm with her fist. Gentle Lamb ran between them, grabbing Violet's hand, then bursting into tears.

"It is okay," Denis explained to her. "She was just pretending. She didn't hurt me."

"But Black Cloud..." she said, then stopped, covering her mouth quickly.

"What about Black Cloud?" Denis asked.

"Nothing," Gentle Lamb said. "Black Cloud is the chief. He can do whatever he wishes."

Her eyes were filled with fear and terror at the mention of her grandfather's name.

"Did Black Cloud hit you?" Denis asked.

"Black Cloud is the chief," she repeated. "He can do whatever he wishes."

"Did he hit your mother?" Denis asked, not the least bit satisfied with her answer.

"Black Cloud is the chief," she said again. "He can do whatever he wishes."

Her big black eyes turned to the ground. Violet could see she was terribly frightened of something. Even though she could not understand their words, she understood her fear. She put her arms around Gentle Lamb, holding her tightly against herself, silently comforting and protecting her.

Denis gently pulled her away from Violet and lifter her chin up to face him. "Did Black Cloud ever hit you?" he repeated.

The fire raged in Denis's eyes. He could see the answer, even though she said again simply, "Black Cloud is the chief. He can do whatever he wishes."

"He might be the chief," Denis said to her, "but he cannot do whatever he wishes. Violet and I will make sure you are never alone with him again. No one will hurt you."

"Not even you?" she asked timidly.

"Never!" Denis shouted. "I would never hurt a child."

Denis then explained the conversation to Violet. She listened intently, holding her tighter and tighter. When he was finished, Violet said "No wonder she doesn't trust men."

"How do you know that?" Denis asked.

"You can see it in her eyes. She wants to trust you. You saved her life, but she is even afraid of you."

"She will learn," Denis said, brushing Gentle Lamb's long thick braid that hung down her back softly with his big callused hand. "In time she will learn that not all men are evil." He smiled broadly at Violet. "Maybe you will learn to trust me too."

"And you will learn that not all Indians are bad," Violet said, jabbing a dagger into Denis's thoughts.

He wondered, as he studied the two women who stood in front of him, how long that would take—for any of them.

"How about some breakfast?" he asked, suddenly anxious to change the subject. "Anybody hungry?"

He repeated the question for Gentle Lamb, and before anyone could answer she was through the big double doors of the hotel and seated at a table.

"I guess that answered that question," Violet said, laughing.

They walked into the dining room together, joining Gentle Lamb. As soon as Mrs. Brown heard them, she came in to see what they wanted to eat. She stood back by the kitchen, studying the curious trio.

"Nice looking family," she said, smiling at them. Then she walked over to take their order. When she left, Gentle Lamb said to him, "Spring Flower is going to take me to the river to wash."

"You call her Spring Flower?" he asked in surprise.

"It is her name," Gentle Lamb explained. "I told her my name and asked her hers. She drew a picture of a purple violet. That is a spring flower. Her name is Spring Flower."

Denis squeezed her shoulder affectionately, then told Violet what she had just said.

"I like it," Violet said. "I am glad to be Spring Flower."

"How did she know you were going to take her to the river to wash?"

Violet related the story of trying to get her to wash up in the room, and how she had drawn a picture of someone in the river.

"But how did she know that you were going to take her there?" he asked.

"Simple," Violet said. "I drew a sunset on her picture."

He nodded his head, delighted with both of his companions. "I said you were both smart," he said.

Violet felt her face turn as red as Gentle Lamb's. She had to learn to handle his compliments as well as she did his complaints.

CHAPTER 8

"I want to fulfill my promise to you," Denis said as they finished their breakfast.

"What promise?" Violet asked.

"To my knowledge," Denis said, grinning, "I only made one."

"I'm sorry," Violet said. "So much has happened, I'm afraid I don't remember." When he didn't elaborate she asked, "Would you remind me, please?"

"Maybe I will just let you wonder," he teased.

"Come on!" Violet pleaded. "Tell me. Please."

"And if I don't?" Denis asked.

"Then I guess I'll have to drag it out of you," she responded, pulling on his jacket.

"No!" Gentle Lamb yelled. She raced to Violet and pulled her away from Denis. She began talking to him, leaving Violet in the dark once again.

The poor thing, Violet thought. What have people done to her to make her so jumpy and nervous? They were just teasing each other, playfully jesting. It appeared that she had never had fun with anyone. She didn't know how to react to such hanky-panky.

Denis explained to her that Violet couldn't remember that he was going to take her to meet the families in the village, and that she was trying to pull the information out of him. Much to Violet's relief, Gentle Lamb began to laugh, then said something else to Denis. It was obvious he was her hero.

Violet smiled at the two of them. There was a certain charm about him that seemed to bring out the best—or the worst—in a person. In Gentle Lamb's case it was the best; in hers, it was the worst.

"She thinks I should tell you," Denis finally said to Violet. "I told you we would go meet the other families in the village. We didn't get very far yesterday."

"I'm ready whenever you are," she said, getting up from the table. "I need a good walk to work off all those hotcakes anyway."

"They look just fine on you," Denis said, winking at her. "In fact, I do believe anything would look fine on you. Just fine, indeed."

The threesome made their way from house to house, meeting the women and children in each residence.

"There is only one left," Denis said, pointing to a large frame house with a lovely porch on the front of the edifice. "It is the Bowen house. I saved the best for last."

"And why is it the best?" Violet asked.

"You will see when you meet Mrs. Bowen. I just know you will like her."

They walked in the direction of the house, talking as they went.

"Did you ask the people if they wanted a school here before you wrote to me?" Violet asked.

Denis sensed that she was nervous about something. He had not noticed anything particularly amiss in any of the homes. The children, especially, seemed delighted with the prospect of a school of their own.

"Yes," Denis replied. "In fact, we called a town meeting about it. Everyone was in agreement." He reached over and grasped her hand. "You are just nervous because you don't know them yet. You will be fine, just you wait and see." He flashed that big toothy smile at her as he added, "Anybody with any good sense at all would be thrilled to have you here."

"You included?" Violet asked, then turning her face away from him. She had not meant to say that at all.

"Especially me," he said.

"I don't know what it is," Violet said, still pursuing the issue, "but they don't trust me."

"You're just imagining that," Denis said, trying to reassure her. "Wait until you meet Mrs. Bowen. She will make you feel better."

"I hope so," Violet said as they approached the Bowen home. She squeezed Gentle Lamb's hand. She realized that the child had been unusually quiet for some time, but she imagined that she felt as out-of-place as she did herself.

Denis climbed the four wide wooden steps, walked across the porch and knocked on the door. In a matter of seconds a tiny little lady, dressed in an elegant green satin gown, appeared to welcome them.

"It's about time, Mr. McLeod," she said, trying to sound put-out that he had waited so long to bring the new arrival to meet her. The warmth in her voice made both Violet and Gentle Lamb smile immediately.

"Mrs. Bowen," Denis said, reaching out to gather her hand in his. He bowed very formally, kissing her tiny white hand, which Violet noted was sporting a huge diamond ring, the likes of which she had never seen.

"Please come in," she invited. "Led! Fetch some tea. We have guests."

Violet wondered who Led was. The whole atmosphere was one of breeding, and she almost expected a black servant to come out with a pot of tea and crumpets. She had read about such places in the south and in large cities like Boston and Philadelphia, but she never expected anything like this in the wilderness of Minnesota.

In a few minutes a small boy, dressed in a black wool suit, appeared, carrying a tray with a china teapot, a matching sugar bowl and creamer, three tiny demitasse cups and a plate of freshly baked sugar cookies.

Mrs. Bowen poured the tea herself, handing a cup to Violet, one to Denis and then taking one herself.

"Led, why don't you take the little girl out into the kitchen and get some milk for the two of you? You may have some cookies as well."

"Yes, ma'am," he said respectfully. "Come on, Wenona," he said, leading the way into the kitchen.

Gentle Lamb stopped dead in her tracks. She began to talk to Led, and much to Violet's surprise, Led answered her in her own tongue.

"Mother," Led said, taking Gentle Lamb by the hand and leading her to Mrs. Bowen, "may I present Gentle Lamb to you?

She has been given a new name. Mr. McLeod gave it to her. It is a pretty name, don't you think, Mother?"

Mrs. Bowen stretched her own hand out to Gentle Lamb. "I think it is a beautiful name. Will you please tell her that I think Mr. McLeod chose wisely?"

Led relayed the message to Gentle Lamb. She smiled at Mrs. Bowen, then surprised them all with a very clearly-spoken "Thank you."

"Where did she learn that?" Mrs. Bowen asked.

"Since she is living with me, I have taught her some English words," Violet explained.

"That is lovely," Mrs. Bowen said, "but why is the child staying with you?"

"You heard about Rattling Leaf and Little Flower?" Denis asked.

"Of course," Mrs. Bowen said.

"Gentle Lamb is the chief's granddaughter, Little Flower's sister. When they died she was forced to run away. I found her all curled up at the top of Maiden Rock."

"Oh!" Mrs. Bowen said, clapping her hand over her mouth in horror. "How awful! The poor child! She must have been frightened to death."

"She was," Denis said. "It took a long time for her to finally come down. Then I had to carry her."

Violet chuckled. "Denis gave her the new name Gentle Lamb, but she also gave him an Indian name: Arms-of-Steel."

Mrs. Bowen studied Denis a few moments, then remarked, "I do believe it is quite appropriate."

"So do I," Violet said. She supposed Mrs. Bowen had also heard about her own wet arrival in Lake City, and she prayed that it would not be brought up. It was embarrassing enough the first time, without having to relive it.

In an attempt to avoid the subject she asked, "How is it that your son knows the Sioux language?"

"My husband believes that everything a person can learn will benefit him in some way. He says if the Indians survived here for who knows how many years before the white man came, they must be smarter than most people give them credit for. When we first arrived there were hardly any children here for Led to play with except the Dakotas, so he began to learn their ways—and their language."

"That is wonderful!" Violet exclaimed. "Wouldn't it be wonderful if we could get some of the Indian children to teach us all some of their language?"

"How would you do that, my dear?" Mrs. Bowen asked.

"We could make it a part of the classroom work. We could study both English and Dakota."

"The people are called Dakota," Mrs. Bowen said, correcting Violet gently. "When it is the spoken language it is called Sioux."

"Sioux," Violet said, repeating the word to firmly plant it in her mind. "Anyway, that way the children would learn Sioux, and the Indian children would learn English. Just think how much easier life here would be if we could all communicate with one another."

"I think you are dreaming of heaven," Mrs. Bowen said. "The Indians will never allow their children to attend a white man's school. Even if they would, the white people would never stand for it. They would close the school down first."

"I don't understand," Violet said. "Why?"

"The white people think they are far superior to the Indians," Mrs. Bowen stated, "and the Indians do not trust the white man. Their ways are all so foreign to them."

"But Led..." Violet said.

"Unfortunately," Mrs. Bowen said, "not everyone has Arnold Bowen for a father."

"But why is he so different?" Violet asked.

"You obviously haven't met Arnold Congdon Bowen yet," Mrs. Bowen said, smiling knowingly at Denis. "When you do, you will see."

They talked for some time while they sipped their tea and ate their cookies, then Violet said she really should be getting back to the hotel.

"You are living at the hotel?" Mrs. Bowen asked.

"Yes," Violet replied. "It seemed the best thing for the time being."

"I have extra rooms here," she offered, "if you would like to rent one of them..."

"That is very kind," Violet said, "but I don't want to be a burden to anyone."

"Burden?" Mrs. Bowen said, laughing. "My dear, it would be such a joy to have someone around here with whom I could share some girl talk. Arnold gets up early in the morning and leaves for his work. He builds houses, you know. He doesn't come home until it is dark outside. Of course in the winter time that makes quite a short day, but in the summer... Why, it is very lonely with just Led to talk to."

"But Gentle Lamb?" Violet said, a question in her voice.

"She would be welcome here as well," Mrs. Bowen said. "I'm sure Led would be glad to have someone his own age to play with instead of trying to find ways to entertain his mother."

Violet was almost ready to accept when she caught a warning glance from Denis.

"Perhaps you should discuss it with Mr. Bowen first."

"That I will do," Mrs. Bowen assured her, "but when he says 'Yes' you will have no choice but to agree to the offer."

"If he agrees," Violet said, "I shall gladly accept. Now, I really must be on my way."

She stood up and shook Mrs. Bowen's hand. "It has been most delightful meeting you, Mrs. Bowen," she said sincerely.

"Likewise," Mrs. Bowen responded.

~*~

As they wound their way back to Browns' Hotel, Violet asked Denis about the Bowens.

"Mrs. Bowen is the granddaughter of William Alexander. Her maiden name was Mary Jane Alexander."

Violet looked at him blankly.

"Am I supposed to know who William Alexander is?" she asked.

"Only if you are from New York, I suppose," Denis said. "He was George Washington's aide-de-camp, his right-hand man, during the Revolution. He was the next thing to royalty that this country has ever known. He had a British title: Lord Stirling. His family owned Stirling Castle in Scotland, the place where Mary, Queen of Scots had her coronation. William Alexander, Mrs. Bowen's grandfather, married Sarah Livingston, the sister of Robert Livingston, the most noted attorney this country has ever known."

Violet was speechless for several moments. "But how did she end up in Lake City, Minnesota?" she asked when she regained her voice.

"She married Arnold Bowen, and he had a flair for adventure, like most everyone else who ended up here."

"You are right," Violet said. "I do like her. I hope Mr. Bowen likes me. It would be wonderful to live with such a woman! And just think of the things Gentle Lamb could learn."

Neither of them had been paying much attention to Gentle Lamb, who had skipped on ahead. Now they could hear her reciting something over and over again. They listened more carefully.

"I like you! I like you!" she repeated over and over again in perfect English.

Denis asked her if she knew the meaning of what she was saying. Her eyes lit up like evening stars as she told Denis—in Sioux—what it meant.

"It seems that we have a young romance budding," he said to Violet. "Led taught her to say that in English and he learned it in Sioux. He told her that she is never to forget, no matter what anyone tells her or does to her, that he likes her."

"Young love!" Violet sighed as they walked into the hotel.

Mrs. Brown smiled, assuming that she knew exactly what was developing. She watched Denis's eyes as they followed Violet ascending the stairs to her room.

"Wonderful, isn't it?" she mused to herself, too softly for Denis to hear.

~*~

Violet was surprised to unlock the door to her hotel room and find Rose Petal on her bed, bouncing up and down, just like Gentle Lamb had done.

Gentle Lamb ran to her mother and they hugged so tightly Violet wondered if they would ever let go of each other. The two chattered excitedly, then Rose Petal pulled on the pouch that hung around her waist, opened it, took a beautiful beaded necklace out and put it around Gentle Lamb's neck.

Gentle Lamb handled it carefully, her eyes shining brightly and the grin on her face reaching from ear to ear. She went over to the paper Violet had set out for her and looked at Violet as she picked up the ink and pen and asked something, which Violet assumed was asking permission to use it. Violet nodded, then watched as Gentle Lamb drew two little girls, one slightly larger than the other one. She drew a necklace on the smaller girl.

Violet knew instinctively that it was Little Flower and Gentle Lamb. She pointed to each of them and said their names. Gentle Lamb beamed proudly as she repeated the names in English, something Led had taught her earlier in the afternoon.

Gentle Lamb reached out and took her mother's index finger and pointed to the smaller girl in the picture, then said something, then "Little Flower." Rose Petal slowly repeated it.

"Yes!" Gentle Lamb squealed with delight as she wrapped her arms around her mother's neck. She moved away quickly and pointed to the other girl. "Gentle Lamb," she said.

"Gen-tle Lamb," Rose Petal repeated.

"Yes!" Gentle Lamb said, and she was joined by Violet's enthusiastic "Yes!"

Gentle Lamb once again took up the pen and dipped it into the ink bottle. She scribbled over Little Flower's necklace and drew it on the picture of herself, then she reached up and ran her hands over the necklace her mother had put on her neck.

Suddenly, outside, on the street below, they heard a horrible bellow. Violet went to the window, and there was Black Cloud, screaming and walking up and down the road, back and forth.

Rose Petal recognized the roar of her husband and she rushed to the door, running down the back stairway, going behind the buildings so she could quietly sneak into their teepee and wait for Black Cloud to calm down and return home.

Violet, sensing danger, took Gentle Lamb downstairs and asked Mrs. Brown if she would watch the girl for a little while until Black Cloud had settled down.

Mrs. Brown took Gentle Lamb by the hand and led her to a high wooden stool. She lifted her onto it, then went over to the cupboard to cut a big slice of cake for her. She set the cake at the table where she was busy preparing food for the evening meal, then she pushed the stool over beside the table.

Gentle Lamb grinned proudly as she reached down and said "fork" as she picked it up and cut off a big bite of the cake.

Violet repeated "fork" as she turned and headed for the stairway and her room. She wondered how long Black Cloud would thunder outside.

CHAPTER 9

Violet was busy preparing for the coming school lessons when Denis appeared at her door, announcing that he was ready to help her move her belongings to the Bowens'. She had only yesterday finished unpacking all of her things, and she hated the thought of putting them all back into the bags to haul them across town.

She waited for Denis to leave, but he walked to the bed and sat down, crossed one leg over the other knee and watched her.

Violet sat at her desk, not moving, just waiting for him to leave, which it appeared he was not apt to do.

"Well, aren't you going to pack?" he finally asked.

"No," she said, trying to concentrate on her lessons but aware of his overbearing presence.

He jumped up and walked over beside her. He pulled her up and spun her around so she was staring right straight at him.

"You are the most exasperating woman I've ever known in my life!" he shouted at her.

"Oh, and you are such a wonderful judge of character. We have known each other"—she glanced at the watch that hung around her neck—"almost thirty whole hours now!"

"Some things don't require a lot of time," he said. "Now pack, woman!"

"I'll pack when I'm good and ready to," she said. "Gentle Lamb is downstairs with Mrs. Brown, and I'm sure she will help me when she gets back. We can manage quite well without you, thank you very much. You may leave now."

She marched to the door, opened it and stood there waiting for him to leave. At long last he picked up his hat and walked out the door.

"Some schoolmarm you are," he sputtered as he left. "Sure hope you have more patience with the children than you do with me."

"And I hope the children know how to behave themselves better than you do," she retorted.

He walked down the hall, saying as he went, "You can carry all your own bags all the way across town. See if I care."

~*~

Violet relented and ran out into the hall, calling out to him. "All right, I'm sorry. Will you come back for a few minutes? There is something I need to know."

Denis stopped, turning around slowly, then asked, "And just why should I? You just ordered me to leave."

"I said I'm sorry." She waited, wondering why indeed he should do anything she asked of him. She really had not been very kind to him. In fact, she admitted to herself, she had never before treated anyone so shabbily. Uncle King and Aunt Caroline would be horrified if they knew how she had behaved. They had certainly not raised her that way.

"It's about Gentle Lamb," she said, hoping that would offer the incentive to come back and listen. To her relief, he headed back towards her. When they got inside her room, Violet was careful to keep the door ajar lest anyone might have seen him enter. She knew how gossip spread in small towns, and she was certain Lake City was no exception.

Denis plopped down on the bed and Violet turned the chair from her small desk so she was facing him. She weighed where to begin. She felt certain that Denis would do anything within his power to protect Gentle Lamb. He had already proven that when he rescued her from Maiden Rock.

"When Wenona—Gentle Lamb—and I came back here from the Bowens, there was someone waiting inside for us."

Denis looked aghast. "You didn't lock your door?"

"Of course I did," Violet snapped at him, insulted that he would think she was that careless. "I don't know how she got in, but that's not the important issue."

"Well, are you going to tell me who it was, or am I supposed to guess?"

"It was Rose Petal," Violet said, her voice so low Denis had to strain to hear her.

"Rose Petal came here? Do you realize she might have been risking her very life by doing that? If Black Cloud finds out..."

Violet could almost hear the thoughts churning in his mind.

"But why?" Denis asked.

"She had something for Gentle Lamb." Violet turned sideways on her chair so she could reach her desk. She took the picture Gentle Lamb had drawn of the two girls and handed it to Denis. He studied it carefully for a couple of minutes.

"I don't understand this," he said finally.

"This," Violet said, pointing to the necklace, first on Little Flower and then to Gentle Lamb. "Rose Petal gave Gentle Lamb a beautiful beaded necklace."

"So she is not willing to declare Gentle Lamb anathema in spite of Black Cloud's order," Denis said, more to himself than to Violet. "She is in danger. Black Cloud has a violent temper."

"Do you think he would really hurt his own daughter?" Violet asked.

"In a split second," Denis said convincingly. "He's done it before. That's why Rose Petal is alone."

"Alone?" Violet asked.

"Yes. Her husband, Rising Water, was supposedly hurt in a hunting accident, but we all knew better. We knew Black Cloud was behind it, but we could not prove that the arrow came from his bow."

"But why?" Violet asked, shaking her head in dismay.

"Several people saw them in a fight just hours before a party went hunting, but nobody would say anything about it and no one seemed to know what it was about."

"But to try to kill his own son-in-law..."

"Black Cloud's word is law to the tribe," Denis explained. "Every member of the tribe knows better than to cross him—or they should know."

As fast as the change from a brilliant orange sky at night to total darkness at sunset, Denis changed the subject.

"The necklace—did Rose Petal say anything about it?"

"Well, yes, to Gentle Lamb, but I have no idea what it was." She thought a few moments, then said, "Rose Petal took her hand and placed it over Gentle Lamb's heart."

"A giveaway," Denis said. "Wikpeyapi."

"A giveaway?" Violet asked.

"Yes," Denis said. "This might take awhile to explain to you." He shifted his position a bit to get comfortable. "When a member of the tribe dies, they often have something that was very special to them that they leave behind for a family member or a close friend. It makes sense that Little Flower would leave a giveaway for her sister. On the other hand, perhaps Rose Petal made the decision for Little Flower, since she couldn't decide it for her herself."

Denis got up and walked to the window. He had seen—and heard—Black Cloud bellowing earlier. He was glad he was gone, for Gentle Lamb's sake, but he wondered if Rose Petal was safe. The thought that he appeared concerned about "one of them" brought a smile to Violet's face. He could act as hard-hearted as he wanted to, but the more she saw of him the more she realized how tender he was just beneath the surface.

"It appears that Black Cloud is gone. Let's go down and get Gentle Lamb and bring her back up here with us," Denis said.

"Why don't you go get her and I'll start packing?"

Pleased with her condescension to do what he had suggested earlier, he vanished.

~*~

Violet was busy putting her belongings into the cloth bags she had just finished emptying the day before when Denis and Gentle Lamb returned. She had left the door open, so they walked right in. She smiled as she saw them swinging their clutched hands back and forth high into the air.

"Knife, fork, spoon, cake, milk..." Gentle Lamb repeated several times.

She will be easy to teach, Violet thought.

Once they were inside the room, Gentle Lamb sat on the bed, again bouncing up and down. "Bed," she said, waiting for Violet's approval, which she got with a big hug.

"Tell her I am proud of her," she instructed Denis, which he did.

"Thank you," Gentle Lamb said.

"You're welcome," Violet replied, forming the words slowly for Gentle Lamb.

"You wel-come," Gentle Lamb repeated.

"Close enough," Violet said, smiling warmly at her.

"Hmph!" Denis grumbled. "If I make an error, or if little Henry does, you are so quick to correct us."

"That's different," Violet said. "You should know better."

"Knowing and doing, that's two different things," Denis said.

"Different things," Gentle Lamb aped.

Denis repeated the words for her in Sioux so she would know what they meant.

Gentle Lamb nodded, smiling at him.

Denis reached over and gently ran his fingers over Gentle Lamb's necklace.

"Wikpeyapi?" he asked.

Gentle Lamb nodded, smiling at him, then added something else.

"She says Little Flower lives on in her," Denis explained to Violet. "It is, as I told you, a giveaway."

"Tejuta hugmiya?" Denis asked Gentle Lamb, and again, she nodded.

"It is a medicine wheel," Denis said to Violet. "It is a round circle, and the cross in the middle is the four colors of the wind: white, red, yellow and black. You cannot find the beginning or the end to the circle."

Violet walked over and studied the necklace closely, trying to find any sort of a seam or a knot or a break in the ring. She shook her head. "How do they do that?" she asked Denis. "I can't find one."

"Once it is completed," Denis said, "no one can, not even the person who made it."

"But how..." Violet asked, a puzzled look on her face.

"Magic," Denis said, grinning.

Violet smiled back at him. She wanted to tease him about being so soft-hearted, in spite of his claims to the contrary. She held back, however. There was no sense jinxing a good thing.

"Grandmothers usually make the medicine wheel for their grandchildren for the Hunka ceremony. That is when a young child is given their permanent name."

"But why was Little Flower given her name before Gentle Lamb?" Violet inquired. "Isn't Gentle Lamb older than Little Flower?"

"It has nothing to do with age," Denis said, scratching his head as he tried to explain traditions of ages and generations past. The Indian ways were so complex. "The child is given a lifetime name when the grandfathers reveal it to the parents—or to the chief."

"For some reason that I don't understand, Gentle Lamb has always been an outcast to Black Cloud, even before he sent her away."

"Because she played with the white children?" Violet asked.

"That certainly didn't help," Denis said, "but it began long before that."

"Does she know that?" Violet asked.

"I'm sure she does. Black Cloud has made no secret of it—to anyone."

"The poor thing," Violet said, putting her arm around Gentle Lamb and giving her a big squeeze. She was delighted when Gentle Lamb wrapped her arms around her and returned the hug.

"See the feathers on the necklace?" Denis asked, turning his attention back to the giveaway.

Violet nodded.

"Eagles are a sign of good fortune, prosperity and life. This is an eagle feather," he said, touching them. "Boys get a regular feather and girls get a longer plume. To an Indian, it signifies good health in the person's life. That is why they call it a 'medicine wheel.' The white man thinks it looks like a halo encircling a cross."

"Thank you for explaining all of that to me," Violet said, placing her hand on Denis's arm. She felt a tingle as her body touched his, causing her to jump. "I have to get my things packed," she said. "I'll send word to you when I—we—are ready to go over to the Bowens'." She went to the door and waited for him to leave.

Denis walked out into the hall, calling back, "Goodbye, Gentle Lamb" as he walked away.

"Goodbye, Denis," Gentle Lamb called back to him.

"I do good?" she asked Violet.

"You do very good," Violet said, for once ignoring the proper grammatical structure of her sentence. For a beginner, she did very good.

~*~

It was late in the afternoon before Violet was finally ready to head across town to her new home. She had informed Aunt Caroline of her decision, as well as Mrs. Brown. They both seemed pleased for her, although she sensed that Aunt Caroline had hoped she would be living with them, making it easier for the care of the boys.

"Ready?" Violet asked Gentle Lamb. She took her pad of paper and drew the closest image of the Bowen house that she could manage. "This is our new home," she tried to explain.

Gentle Lamb looked puzzled.

Violet placed two people in front of the house, one adult and one little girl. "Me," she said, pointing to the woman in the drawing. "Gentle Lamb," she said, pointing to the smaller figure.

Gentle Lamb's face lit up like a brightly burning candle. She took the pencil from Violet and drew a bed inside the frame of the house, then drew a line from the two people to the bed. The expression on her face, her eyebrows highly arched, was a perfect question mark.

"Yes," Violet said, hugging her tightly. "This will be our home. Our bed."

"I like you," Gentle Lamb said, smiling from ear to ear. "Led say 'I like you!'"

"I think you like Led too," Violet said. "Let's go."

Violet placed one bag of her belongings over her shoulder, then picked up the other two bags—one in each hand.

"Me," Gentle Lamb said, taking one of the bags herself. She grunted, almost overwhelmed by the weight and size of the bundle, but pulled it along behind her.

"I'll take it," Violet said, reaching for it.

"Me!" Gentle Lamb insisted.

Violet laughed. "If you want to, but if it gets too heavy I'll take over."

"Me!" Gentle Lamb said again, already at the stairway with the bag. Bump! Bump! Bump! it went as it clattered down the steps.

Hearing the noise, Mrs. Brown came out to see what was happening.

"Why don't you wait until Pa gets back so he can help you carry those things over?" she asked.

"We can manage," Violet said, "especially with such good help." She grinned at Gentle Lamb.

"You're sure?" Mrs. Brown asked.

"Absolutely," Violet assured her.

"We will miss having you here, but with the school starting up before long I'm sure we will keep in touch."

"It's not like Lake City is such a big place," Violet said, laughing. "I'm sure we will see each other often."

"I guess you're right," Mrs. Brown said. "Can you find your way to the Bowens?"

"I was careful to watch which turns to take," Violet said, setting her bag down for a moment. "I was just wondering one thing."

"What's that?" Mrs. Brown asked.

"Denis—Mr. McLeod—said Uncle King would have to build in a certain part of the village, since he was Scotch and that was Little Scotland. Yet he told me that Mrs. Bowen was descended from a Scottish family and they live on the opposite end of town."

"My dear Violet," Mrs. Brown said, obviously as taken with the standing of such a woman as Mary Jane Bowen as Denis was, "if you are an Alexander, you can build anywhere you want to!"

"I see," Violet said, beginning to understand that even in a tiny, crude pioneer village like Lake City there was a certain social status all its own.

~*~

About halfway across town, Violet set the two bags she was carrying on the ground to rest for a few moments. Gentle Lamb, who had pulled her bundle all the way behind her, perched on top of it.

"Can you make it?" Violet asked her, knowing she could not understand many of her words yet, and wishing she had not been so stubborn when it came to Denis's offer of help.

She did not see that behind the trees Denis McLeod was lurking, watching the strong-willed new woman in town who had refused his help.

"Home!" Gentle Lamb said excitedly, pointing to the Bowen's house, which was just barely in view.

"Home," Violet agreed, getting a new surge of energy at the child's enthusiasm.

~*~

It seemed like almost no time when they arrived at the front porch of the Bowen's house. Led, hearing them come, ran to greet them. He took the pack from Gentle Lamb and went ahead of them.

"They're here, Mother," he called out. Mrs. Bowen came out from the kitchen to greet them.

"Welcome home," she said warmly, walking towards the room they would occupy. "You may put your belongings in here. This will be your room, but I insist that you feel free to come and go as you wish in any part of the house."

"Except Mother and Father's bedroom," Led announced. "Nobody goes in there!"

Mrs. Bowen blushed a bright red. True, she had told Led that their room was sacred ground, but even though she and Arnold had been married for almost ten years, their private marital life was just that—private. And, she was quick to admit to herself, it was the best part of life that Lake City had to offer.

Violet pulled the rope free around the top of one of the bags and began to shake out her garments. Instinctively, Gentle Lamb reached in and took out the next item, handing it carefully to her new caretaker.

"Why don't you leave that for a bit?" Mrs. Bowen suggested. "I fancy that you have not even had afternoon tea yet, and there's no proper woman who can survive without her afternoon tea."

Violet tried hard not to laugh. She had never had afternoon tea in her life, with the exception of the one she had yesterday with Mrs. Bowen. She had never thought of what life as a society mistress would be like, but she felt certain that if she was going to remain at the Bowen house for very long she had a lot of things to learn.

Violet took Gentle Lamb by the hand and followed Mrs. Bowen out into the living room.

"Led!" she called, summoning her son. He appeared immediately. Violet wondered if all the children in Lake City were as obedient to their parents as Led Bowen. If so, she had nothing to fear—except, perhaps, Denis McLeod. So far he had shown no signs of cooperation with her. Support? Yes, but cooperation? No. And certainly not obedience. You would think, the way he carried on about the school, he was the one running it, not her. Granted, he had hired her, but she was going to have to have a little chat with him. If he wanted her to do her job, he had to back away and let her do it. After all, she had been trained to do it. And she would, she vowed, do it well.

Violet walked to the plush purple velvet sofa and plopped down on it. She realized just how tired she was. Why was she always so

stubborn? It would have been a lot easier if she had let Denis—
Mr. McLeod—haul her things over to her new home.

Mrs. Bowen stared in disbelief at Violet. She didn't say a word,
but went to her oak rocker, properly puffed her skirt out of the
way and gracefully sat down.

Gentle Lamb, sensing that Mrs. Bowen was showing them the
proper way for a lady to seat herself, stood up, smoothed her
buckskin dress and sat down, as prim and proper as anything you
ever saw. She turned to Violet and pointed. Violet, duly
embarrassed, followed suit. Gentle Lamb placed her hand over
her mouth and giggled.

"She is going to be just fine," Mrs. Bowen said, taking the tea
service from Led as he brought it in. She smiled at Violet. "So, my
dear, are you."

CHAPTER 10

Daily, promptly at three in the afternoon, a different woman arrived at the Bowen home, their children in tow. Mrs. Bowen had taken it upon herself to "entertain" each family in Lake City, hoping to ease the beginning of the school year.

Violet enjoyed the friendship she soon acquired with each of the women, but her primary goal was to get to know the children. If they were comfortable with each other, she was sure, the tears of uncertainty could be avoided.

"Miss Violet Seymour, Mistress of the Lake City Grammar School," Mrs. Bowen introduced her each afternoon as they sat down at the big round oak dining room table, always properly clad with a crisp white linen tablecloth, matching napkins and a perfect floral centerpiece of the flowers which grew in abundance in Mrs. Bowen's backyard flower garden.

Each day, as per her instructions, Led carefully took Gentle Lamb outside to play. Mr. Bowen had even built a private little playhouse in the back, hidden in the trees, for them. Nothing was said about Gentle Lamb at the afternoon teas, but Violet assumed everyone knew that she had taken the orphan under her wings. News travels quickly in a town the size of Lake City.

Almost every evening Denis McLeod stopped by to pay a visit. He kept Violet informed of the progress on the schoolhouse, the time frame of how soon Aunt Caroline and Uncle King would be ready to move into their own home in Little Scotland, the town gossip which he heard at the Browns' Hotel, and always a greeting from his Uncle Lath.

From time to time, always in the morning, Violet would wander over to the Hotel and visit with Mrs. Brown and her family. Aunt Caroline excitedly told her, as they sat over a cup of coffee in the dining room, that not only were they to have their own home, but "Grandpa Benjamin and Grandma Sarrah will have one right next to us, and Charles and his family the one next to them."

"What about Uncle Frederick?" Violet asked, smiling at the thought of the newlyweds trying to keep quiet while they were living with another family.

"He has decided to settle on the other side of the lake," Aunt Caroline said. "Alonzo talked him into it. He says it is much better on the Wisconsin side." She laughed. "He says he can't stand the Minnesota mosquitoes."

"Denis says the school will be ready next week," Aunt Caroline said. She studied Violet carefully. "Are you ready?"

"Yes," Violet said, her voice full of confidence, "I do believe I am."

They were interrupted by Denis McLeod, who promptly sat down with them.

"You are what?" he asked.

"Nose trouble?" Violet asked, a twinkle in her eye. She knew they had nothing to hide, but she did enjoy teasing him. He too often got the upper hand, and she delighted in turning the tables when she got the chance.

"I suppose you could call it that," he said, "but you are in my employ."

"And that gives you a right to know my every thought?" Violet asked.

"Indeed it does," Denis said, sitting more erect than usual. "After all, you are my mistress."

Aunt Caroline and Violet gasped in unison.

"Your what?" Aunt Caroline nearly shouted.

"My mistress," Denis repeated.

"I'll have you know that I am not a mistress—yours or anyone else's!" Violet insisted.

"But Mrs. Bowen, she said you are the Mistress of the Lake City Grammar School." He smiled at her, trying to show his complete innocence. "I always thought a mistress was a—well, you know—a kept woman. But, when I heard Mrs. Bowen call you that, well, I knew I must be wrong. Mrs. Bowen, above anyone else in all of Lake City, would know what is proper."

"It might be proper to be called the mistress of the school," Violet insisted, her face red with both rage and embarrassment, "but it is quite another matter to be called a man's mistress." She glared at him, her eyes so intense they nearly bored a hole right through him. "Especially not yours! I repeat, I am not your mistress."

Aunt Caroline grinned. She remembered how she and King had argued over matters much less complicated than this before they declared their love for each other. Yes, it was as clear as the nose on her face that Violet and Denis were falling in love with each other. She wondered how long it would be before they woke up to that fact.

"I do apologize," Denis said, surprising Violet. He was not, she knew, in the habit of admitting he was wrong. She would have to write this down in her diary. It might be the only time in history it occurred.

Violet hurried to steer the conversation to the school.

"It is so cute!" she said excitedly.

"Cute?" Denis growled. "The dadburned thing is supposed to be practical. Sturdy. Weatherproof. But cute? It isn't cute."

"Well, I think it's cute," Violet insisted. "Don't you, Aunt Caroline?"

"I think it is all of the things you both said. And yes, Mr. McLeod, I hate to disagree with you, but it is cute. With the little cupola on top and the bright red bell just waiting to call the children to classes the first day, it is definitely cute."

"Women!" Denis said, huffing and puffing in disgust as he walked away. "If I live to be a hundred and ten, I'll never figure them out."

Aunt Caroline and Violet laughed. "Sure got rid of him in a hurry, didn't we?" Violet offered. "Now, what did you start to ask me before we were so rudely interrupted?"

"As if you minded the interruption," Aunt Caroline said, teasing Violet.

"I did!" Violet insisted. "We were having a private talk, and he had no right to barge in on it."

"He does have certain rights, if you will think about it a minute," Aunt Caroline said.

"And just what gives him those rights?" Violet asked.

"Well, he did save your life," she reminded her niece.

"You don't have to bring that up again, do you?" Violet remarked. "I don't suppose anyone in the whole town will ever forget my arrival in Lake City, nor let me forget it either."

Aunt Caroline chuckled. "It was rather amusing," she said.

"You were about to say?" Violet asked again, trying to get back to the matters at hand.

"I was just wondering how you were getting along at the Bowens," Aunt Caroline said, showing typical motherly concern.

"Oh, she is just the most wonderful woman!" Violet said. "And Mr. Bowen, he is as amusing as she is proper. And Led, why he is like a little man all grown up. He is so kind to Gentle Lamb."

"But they aren't family," Aunt Caroline said. "If you ever feel you want to move in with us, you know you are always welcome. You are one of our own."

"Thank you," Violet said, getting up and going to the other side of the table and giving her aunt a warm embrace. "I know we are family. I will never forget all you have done for me." Her eyes filled with tears. "Thank you."

"No need to go thanking me," Aunt Caroline said. "Kin folks does as kin folks is."

Violet shuddered slightly. "Do...are," she said under her breath. Honestly, the way the Scottish people butchered the English language! It was no wonder she had decided to become a teacher. Somebody had to set the world straight about such things.

"What do you intend to do about Denis?" Aunt Caroline asked.

"Do about him?" Violet responded, puzzled. "What should I do about him?"

"Well, it seems obvious to me that he is rather stricken with you."

"Stricken?" Violet shrieked. "He's no such thing! He thinks he owns me!"

"Then you will just have to learn how to handle him," Aunt Caroline said. "A woman, if she loves a man, has to let him think he is ruling the household."

"He already thinks he is the Almighty!" Violet said.

"But the secret is, when he is ruling the roost, the woman then learns to rule the rooster!"

Violet stood, pondering her aunt's advice. Suddenly she was hit by the common sense of the words.

"I've got it!" she exclaimed. "You let him think he is running everything, but you use your feminine wiles to persuade him to do whatever you want him to do."

"By George, I think she's got it," Aunt Caroline said, laughing at her niece. "Just be sly about it, and he will soon be wrapped around your little finger."

Violet's face reddened. "And what makes you think I want him wrapped around any part of me?" she asked.

"Woman's intuition," Aunt Caroline said. "Now, I hate to run, but I promised Mrs. B I would help her fix the supper."

"Go ahead," Violet said, "but you're wrong. All wrong."

"We'll see," Aunt Caroline said as she walked out into the kitchen at the Browns' Hotel, clicking her tongue at the surety of the relationship that was growing between her niece and the crafty Denis McLeod.

Violet turned on her heel, nearly tripping on her long full black skirt. She was struggling to keep her balance when a hand reached out and grabbed her by the elbow.

"May I escort you home, Mistress Seymour?" the all-too-familiar voice inquired. He didn't wait for a reply, but fell into step beside her.

CHAPTER 11

Violet sat on the plump overstuffed sofa in the Bowen parlor. Her eyes were fixed on Mrs. Bowen, moving gently back and forth as she pumped on the high oak pump organ she mastered so well. Her face was intent on her music, and Violet smiled as she looked at her reflection in the mirror on the top of the instrument. So perfect and proper, it was amusing to Violet that whenever she played the organ she bit down on her tongue, holding it tightly on first one side of her mouth and then on the other.

"Something amusing?" Mrs. Bowen asked as she spotted Violet's reflection in the mirror when she glanced up.

"Soothing," Violet replied. "It is just what I need."

Mrs. Bowen stopped playing and spun around on the stool she was perched on.

"What is troubling you?" she asked, studying her new boarder.

"I guess I am just nervous about school starting," Violet said. It was true, she was excited about the beginning of her first job, but her real nervousness came from Denis McLeod.

He is so exasperating, she thought. He walks me home, acting like a perfect gentleman. Then he calls me 'mistress,' knowing full well how I loathe the word and all it implies. One minute he is as sweet as honey, and the next instant he is issuing me orders, like I am his property.

"A ha'pence for your thoughts," Mrs. Bowen said, smiling warmly at Violet.

"Just school," she repeated.

Arnold Bowen had come into the room, unnoticed by Violet.

"If I didn't know better, I'd say it was your young suitor," he teased, his long well-groomed mustache curling up at the corners from his grin and his eyes dancing with mischief.

"Now, Arnold!" Mrs. Bowen scolded. "Don't you be putting ideas in the young lady's head."

"As if they aren't already there," he said, winking at Violet.

"I'm sorry, sir," Violet protested, "but I have no suitor—young or old."

"My instincts tell me otherwise," he insisted. "I've seen him come calling on you every evening."

"We have business to discuss," Violet said, placing her hands on her cheeks. They seemed hot to the touch, and she knew they were as red as the embers in the fireplace. "You know full well that it is because of him that I am here. He is sponsoring the school, and since I am the schoolteacher we do have things which must be settled before tomorrow's opening."

"He was interested in the school when Rev. Hazlett was teaching the children too," Arnold Bowen continued, "but I didn't see the two of them meeting together on a daily basis."

"Arnold, that's enough!" Mrs. Bowen said firmly. "You are embarrassing the poor dear."

Arnold dropped the subject immediately. Violet chuckled to herself as she remembered Aunt Caroline's advice earlier in the day. It was obvious that Mrs. Bowen, as tiny and serene as she appeared, had learned the secret well. Arnold Bowen may have been in charge of the Bowen household, but it was as plain as day that Mary Jane Bowen was in control of Arnold Bowen.

Violet reached over to the window ledge beside her and took down the jar of varied-colored sand. She had seen one in every home she had visited in Lake City.

"Pretty, isn't it?" Arnold Bowen asked.

"It is beautiful," Violet agreed, turning it around in her hands and holding it up to the sunlight. The grains of sand seemed to shift from one hue to another as the light changed. "Where does it come from?"

"Denis hasn't yet taken you up to Sugar Loaf?" Arnold asked.

"Sugar Loaf?" Violet asked. He not only hadn't taken her there, he had not even mentioned the place. "Where is that?"

"It's up on the bluffs," Arnold answered. "Come here," he said, walking to the door and standing on the front porch. "There," he said, pointing to the east. "That is Sugar Loaf."

Violet had admired the beautiful bluffs from the first instant she set eyes on them when she was still on the river boat. Denis had described them as magical, and she had to admit he was right. Even the jars of sand seemed to hold unworldly powers.

"I would love to go up there," she said dreamily. "It is the most wonderful place on earth. At least Denis was right about one thing."

"About what, dear?" Mrs. Bowen asked.

"About the bluffs," Violet explained. "He called it Paradise."

Mrs. Bowen laughed. "I suppose Adam and Eve could have stayed out of trouble if God had put them in Lake City instead of in the Garden of Eden."

"Mary Jane, you never cease to amaze me," Arnold said, the fondness for his wife showing in his eyes. "Now why on earth would you say such a thing?"

"Because there are no apple trees here, so they would not have been tempted," she answered. "Isn't that logical?"

They all laughed together at such a summary of the deeper things of life. Arnold didn't have the heart to tell Mrs. Bowen that one of the farms had put in a whole grove of trees a couple of years ago and that they were laden with fruit this year.

Hearing the laughter, Gentle Lamb and Led came running into the house from the playhouse out in back where they spent long hours together.

"What's so funny?" Led asked.

"Your mother," Arnold said.

Led studied his mother carefully. "She's never been especially funny to me," he said, scratching his head. "Why do grownups never make any sense?"

"We make perfect sense," Mrs. Bowen said. "Most of us, anyway. Your father— well, that's quite another matter."

"Funny Mother," Gentle Lamb said in slow, hesitant English.

Violet pulled her onto her lap. "You are learning so much," she said, smoothing her fingers over her long black braids. "I am so proud of you."

"Proud," she repeated, puffing her chest out to its fullest. "Led is proud too."

"I am, Miss Seymour," Led said enthusiastically. "She learns real good."

"Very well," Violet said, correcting his grammar. "I am sorry," she said, realizing that she was not yet in school. The Bowens had taught Led proper etiquette and speech. He was, she thought, entitled to a few slips of the tongue.

"It is quite all right," Mrs. Bowen said. "He knows better, but he does pick up some bad habits from the children he plays with."

Without warning, Gentle Lamb burst into tears and hid her face in Violet's shoulder.

"What is it?" Violet asked. "What is wrong?"

Gentle Lamb said nothing, but kept crying. In no time flat Led was beside her, talking to her in Sioux. Finally Gentle Lamb looked up, dried her tears on her sleeve and smiled faintly.

"What upset her?" Violet asked Led.

"She understood only part of what you said. She has learned a lot of words, and she picks out the ones she recognizes. All she heard was 'bad' 'children' 'he plays with,'" Led explained. "She was afraid you thought she was one of the bad children."

"Please," Violet pleaded with Led, "explain to her that I do not think she is bad. I think she is very good."

Led spoke reassuringly to her, and Gentle Lamb turned to look at Violet, searching for acceptance from her.

"Gentle Lamb is a good girl," Violet said slowly, hoping she would understand. The child's face glowed.

"Mistress Seymour is good girl too," she said.

"Thank you," Violet said, returning her smile and breathing a sigh of relief that they understood each other.

"Would you ask her if she knows how to get to Sugar Loaf?" Violet asked Led.

Led laughed. "Everybody knows how to get to Sugar Loaf, Miss Seymour," Led replied.

"Everyone except me," Violet said. "I would like to go up there."

"Gentle Lamb and I will take you," Led said excitedly.

"That will be nice," Violet said. Before she knew it, the two children had hold of each of her hands and were pulling her out the door.

"Not now," Violet said. "It is too late."

"It is not far," Arnold said. "I will hitch the buggy to the team and take you as far as the foot. From there you will have to walk. It does not take long, and there is nothing more spectacular than watching the sunset or the sunrise from Sugar Loaf."

"I will ride along," Mrs. Bowen said. "It has been far too long since I have visited the bluffs. Perhaps it will do me some good. We will wait for you youngsters while you climb up to the sand ridges. You can take a jar along and fill it so you will have a bit of the bluff of your own. People say it brings good luck."

"I can use all the help I can get," Violet said. Tomorrow would be her first day of school, and she was as nervous as a new kitten being chased by a hound dog. In addition, there was Denis McLeod to deal with. If he continued to think of her as his mistress, she was definitely going to need some good luck! The nerve of the man, anyway!

CHAPTER 12

The buggy bounced along the pathway towards the bluffs. Arnold sat in the front, guiding the horses, with Led at his side. Mrs. Bowen pointed out each farm home as they passed it, giving the vital information on each family.

"That is the Merrills," she said, smiling. "They have seven children. I imagine they will all be in attendance at the school eventually, but the older boys from all the farms will stay home until the harvest is complete."

Violet winced at the idea that such mundane things as crops would take precedence over a valuable education.

"Over yonder is the Webster farm," Mrs. Bowen continued. "They have a whole gaggle of young ones. They will all be in school, even before the crops are in."

"Why is that?" Violet asked.

"They are a proud lot," she explained. "They claim to be descended from Noah Webster himself. Why, when Hattie Webster wanted to marry Zeke Cunningham the whole clan was up in arms."

"I don't understand," Violet said, waiting for an explanation.

"It was really quite simple," Mrs. Bowen elaborated. "Old Zeke couldn't read a word. Couldn't even write his own name. Even his deed carries an 'X' where his name ought to be."

"So?" Violet asked.

"So they forbid them from marrying. 'No Webster will ever marry someone who doesn't know his ABCs,' Bailey Webster decreed loudly from the courthouse steps. 'Words are the foundation of our country, right from the Declaration of Independence to the Emancipation Proclamation!' he shouted. 'No daughter of mine will ever disgrace the name of Webster by marrying an illiterate fool!' And that's the way I suspect it will be until the end of time. So, mark my words, the whole Webster crew will be at the school come morning, even before the doors are open."

Violet laughed. "I hope I am up to the challenge," she said.

"I'm certain of it," Mrs. Bowen said. "You'll do yourself proud at the new school."

Violet looked to the side and gasped, nearly losing her breath. She had never seen such a sight. The hills ahead of them were even more splendid up close than they were from a distance.

"This is Sugar Loaf," Arnold called back to them as he drew the horses to a halt. "It's getting late. If you want to catch the best view of the sunset you'd better be getting a move on."

Violet was out of the buggy in record time. She hurried to catch up with Gentle Lamb and Led as they scrambled up the rocky cliffs. She held her long full skirts up, unconcerned that her ankles were exposed above her high-top button shoes. She didn't want to miss a second of the vision that lay ahead of her.

~*~

Arnold and Mrs. Bowen were sitting in the buggy, watching Violet and the youngsters become smaller and smaller as they climbed higher. Mrs. Bowen, "no bigger than a minute," as Arnold told her, rested her head on Arnold's chest.

"Mary Jane, you are truly a marvel," he said, placing his arm around her tightly.

"What did I do now?" she asked.

"You took our new schoolmarm in and made her feel like part of our family. Then, as if that wasn't enough, you allowed Gentle Lamb to live beneath our roof as well."

"We have always rented the extra room out," she said.

"But you have to know the townfolk are talking," he said.

"Why, Arnold Bowen! I have never known you to be concerned about gossip—about you or anyone else."

"I didn't say I was concerned," he said, "but I know your family. If they knew you had a Redskin living in your own house they'd probably scalp you themselves."

"So we don't tell them," she said, grinning up at him.

"I declare, you are becoming more and more of a Bowen every day."

"And I'm proud of it," she said. "You have taught me a great deal, my dear."

Secure in the knowledge that they were alone, Arnold leaned over and passionately kissed his wife, whom he still called his bride.

"Nice evening, isn't it?" Denis McLeod asked, causing them to pull apart quickly.

"We didn't hear you come up," Arnold said. "You could cause a chap's heart to fail."

"And you could give us all a few lessons on affairs of the heart," Denis teased.

"What brings you out this way?" Arnold asked.

"As if you didn't know," he said. "Mrs. Witherspoon said Violet and the children had headed out towards Sugar Loaf. She failed to mention that you had gone with them."

"If I didn't know better, I would think she was playing matchmaker," Arnold said.

"And Mrs. Witherspoon is the only one?" Mrs. Bowen asked, winking at her husband.

"Our—er—relationship is purely a business one," Denis said, quick to defend his actions. "We needed a schoolmarm, and I decided to find one. There is nothing more to it than that."

"From the way I hear it told," Arnold said, "you consider her your mistress!"

Damn! He should have known his use of that word would come back to haunt him. Violet had pleaded with him not to use it. He was sure she would not have told them about their argument over it, so where would they have gotten such an idea? He never meant anything by it. Certainly not what people were assuming.

"You don't have to look so puzzled," Arnold said. "Gentle Lamb came home one day calling her Mistress Seymour. I asked her where she had learned that word, and she said it is what you call Spring Flower. She said she can tell you like her, and if you call her that, then she will call her that too."

"Guess I'd better watch my step," Denis said, embarrassed by the impression he had given not only the Bowens, but Gentle Lamb as well.

"Reckon so," Arnold said, delighted at the obvious discomfort he had caused the young man. That was the first sign of a sure romance ahead, as far as he was concerned. And two such fine young people deserved each other.

~*~

Violet, Gentle Lamb and Led reached the top of Sugar Loaf. The top, which looked like a peak from a distance, was actually a flat mesa. Violet sat down on the sandy surface and began to slowly and deliberately twist the laces on her hightop shoes free of the hooks. She tugged on the boot and sat, wiggling her toes inside her wool stockings, wishing they were off too.

"Turn around," she ordered Led.

Led, accustomed to immediate obedience, faced away from her. She quickly pulled her stockings off and tucked them into her bodice so they would not get lost or blow away.

"Okay," she told the lad, "you can turn around again. He smiled at her as he watched her squiggle her bare toes into the brightly colored sand, the granules sifting through them.

"It feels good," Violet said. "Do you like the feel of the sand too?"

Led's face colored slightly. Even at his young age, he had never allowed a woman to see his bare feet. Such things just were not allowed at the Bowen household. After all, they had a responsibility to the rest of Lake City, his mother had often told him. He could hear her voice now. "How will anyone ever know how to behave themselves properly if the Alexanders don't show them?"

"I—I don't rightly know," he finally replied.

"You've never felt this wonderful warm sand on your bare feet?" she asked, amazed at the thought. She glanced over at Gentle

Lamb, who had followed her example and had shed her moccasins and was doing exactly as Violet was doing.

"I think it is time you learn how to enjoy life," Violet said, waiting for Led to remove his shoes. When he didn't, Violet grabbed him and got him down on her lap.

"Take off his shoes," Violet instructed Gentle Lamb, pointing to Led's shoes so she would understand what she was saying.

Gentle Lamb grabbed his shoe, unloosed it and pulled it from Led's foot while Violet held him securely. When his shoes and socks were off, Gentle Lamb playfully took a handful of sand and ground it into his bare foot.

"Isn't that wonderful?" Violet asked.

"I must admit," Led confessed, "it does feel good."

They stayed atop the bluff as the sun quickly sank below the horizon. The hues of the sky seemed to match the tones of the sand. Yes, Denis McLeod was definitely right about at least one thing: this was pure magic. If only he was here to share it with me, she thought, then tried to erase the idea from her mind. She had enough problems, what with school starting tomorrow, without focusing her attention on someone as changeable—and probably fickle, she decided—as Denis McLeod.

"We should probably return to Mother and Father," Led said after awhile. "Once the sun is down, it gets dark very quickly."

Violet opened the jar Mrs. Bowen had given her and began to scoop handfuls of sand into it. The children giggled at her as she hurried to get it to the jar before it filtered through her fingers. At last the jar was full. She replaced the lid and stuck the jar into her shoe. With the shoes in hand, they began their descent, carefully, lest they slip.

As they neared the bottom, Violet saw that there was someone else there waiting for them besides Arnold and Mrs. Bowen. Before she could ask who it was, Gentle Lamb exclaimed, "It's Arms-of-Steel!"

Violet shivered, but she knew it was not from the sudden chill that filled the air after the sun had gone down. It was a shiver of fear, of anticipation, of anxiety. A shiver of thrill and delight. A shiver which grew as Denis came to meet them.

"Was it everything I promised?" he asked, his eyes twinkling at the pleasure he saw on her face.

"Oh, it was beautiful!" Violet said. "It is, indeed, Paradise."

"It is, now that you are a part of it," Denis said just softly enough for her to hear and the children not to hear.

Violet turned her face away from him. He had no right to say such a thing to her. She had made it perfectly clear that he had no claims on her—except where the school was concerned.

"Why did you come out here anyway?" she stammered.

"I have a surprise for you," he said. "I am riding back into town with you."

"That is your idea of a surprise?" Violet mocked. "I'm thrilled."

"Come down off your high horse," he chided. "No, I am going to take you to your surprise. Let's hurry."

Violet couldn't stop herself. She smiled at him. She had never seen him so excited, so filled with anticipation. He was like a little child who had made something special for his mother for Mother's Day and was waiting for her reaction.

"Okay, let's go," Violet said, climbing into the buggy. Suddenly she realized that she still had her shoes in her hand and her stockings in her—well, where they shouldn't be. She felt naked, standing there in front of Denis without all of her essentials in place, but there was no graceful way to correct the situation now.

CHAPTER 13

With everyone engaged in busy conversation about the beauty of Sugar Loaf, the fine weather they were having and the excitement of the first day of school so close at hand, Violet had not even noticed that they were approaching the lane which turned off the main path and wound its way to the school until she heard Arnold shout "Whoa!" to the team.

"Why are we at the school?" she asked just as Denis came to greet them. He had ridden on ahead, which Violet had noticed from time to time as she sought for him.

"I told you I have a surprise for you," he said, his eyes dancing with glee. He reached up to take her hand and help her down. He smiled delightedly as he realized that she still had bare feet. He wondered if the rest of her was as cute as her short little turned-up toes. He debated about saying something to her, but felt uneasy about it so he decided to leave well enough alone. After all, he thought, the town already knows she is slightly unorthodox after the splash she made her first day in town.

The group walked to the quaint log building. Violet put her hand out and stopped them.

"Oh, look!" she squealed delightedly. "The shutters are open. And there are windows! Out of real glass! Oh, it is wonderful!"

"Arnold had them sent from Chicago," Mrs. Bowen said proudly. She didn't add that it had taken three tries before they arrived without any breakage.

Violet smiled warmly at the proper-looking man. She wished she could tell him how much such an effort meant to her. "Thank you," was all she could muster.

Arnold and Mrs. Bowen, Denis, Led and Gentle Lamb all waited while Violet visually surveyed the school. No one said a word, but waited to see how long it would take. Finally, as she lifted her eyes upwards, she again shouted in glee. "It even has a school bell!"

"And I want to be the first one to ring it," Led insisted. "I will come early tomorrow morning just to be sure."

"Betcha Willie Webster gets there first!" Arnold said, teasing his son.

"Yeah," Led grumbled, "and Josie too."

"But you were the first one to speak up," Violet told Led, "so the honors belong to you."

"Thank you, Mistress Seymour," he said politely. Then he turned to Denis and winked, saying, "Why don't you go on inside and look it over?"

"Is it really all finished?" Violet asked. It had been little more than a week since she had arrived, and she knew almost every able-bodied man in town had been working on the construction, but this was more than she had ever dared to hope for.

"See for yourself," Denis said, guiding her up the four steps to the front door. She waited for him to open it, but he stood, waiting for her to do it herself. Some gentleman! she thought.

"Surprise!"

Violet looked around the room, stunned. As she glanced from one face to the next she realized that every person in town must be there. At least every white person, she decided as she studied the reaction on Gentle Lamb's face. That she was in the minority—a minority of one—was too obvious.

Almost as if he could read her thoughts, Led took Gentle Lamb's hand in his and said softly, "If anybody says anything, you are with me." He puffed his chest up like that very fact made him the proudest person there.

Violet nodded at him, smiling. She continued to look around at the school. Her school! Her very first school! Hanging from the ceiling was a huge banner which read "WELCOME, MISTRESS SEYMOUR!"

As she gazed at the sign she wondered, Why does it make me so uncomfortable when Denis calls me 'Mistress,' yet when the other people in town used the same exact name it seems like an honor?

"Like your surprise?" Denis asked, shaking her from her wandering mind.

"I love it!" she said excitedly. "Who was behind all this?"

"Your boss," Uncle King called out from one corner. "It was Denis McLeod's idea."

"But we all thought it was a jim-dandy," Thomas Brown added. "As the mayor of Lake City, Mistress Seymour, may we all take this opportunity to give you an official welcome to our fine town. Here's to our new schoolmarm!" he chanted, lifting an imaginary glass into the air for the toast.

The entire group applauded loudly. Violet felt her face turning crimson. She had never been the center of attention for anything. Most times the only reason anybody took this much notice of a female it was because she was getting married. Either that, or she'd died. Well, she could pinch herself, but she was pretty sure she was still alive. And she knew she wasn't anybody's bride, so it must be because of her chosen profession.

"Speech! Speech!" people began calling out to her.

Violet looked down at the floor, then raised her head again. The first face she saw—it seemed like the only face that was there—belonged to the handsome dark-haired Denis McLeod. If she could pretend like he wasn't really there, that she was talking to the other people, maybe she could tell him what was really in her heart—at least part of it. The rest of it would have to wait for some other time. Sometime when she was sure what it really was.

"I am extremely proud to be Lake City's first schoolteacher," Violet said. "I will devote myself fully to the most precious thing you all possess: your children. In the short time I have been here I have met most of you, and I have gotten to know many of the children already. I do not promise to be perfect, but I promise to give them my best." She paused, looked Denis square in the eyes, and said, "And I sincerely thank you for all you have done to make this day possible."

Again a loud cheer went up from the crowd. Then the cry changed to Thomas Browns' thundering announcement: "Let's eat!"

Violet stared at the sumptuous potluck feast that was set on the table at the back of the school room. Denis came over to her and led her to form the line. "The guest of honor always goes first," he said.

Violet chose a plate from the stack and began to fill it with the wonderful smelling delicacies. Denis watched in awe. Thomas Brown was right, he thought. How does such a little bit of a thing, with all the right things in just the right places, manage to put so much food away?

"You're welcome," he said, referring to the comment at the end of her speech. "I'd do it all over again, if I could."

CHAPTER 14

At the end of the evening, Violet sighed deeply as she stood with the last few stragglers, too exhausted to really hear what they were saying.

"If you don't mind," Denis said to Arnold Bowen, "I would like to escort Mistress Seymour home."

"I'm quite sure it will be fine," Arnold said, grinning knowingly. "That is, if she approves. Violet?" he asked.

She ignored him, unaware that he was addressing her.

"Miss Seymour?" Arnold asked, gazing at her in admiration. For such a young upstart, he thought, she definitely has spunk. She handled herself like a true professional tonight, even with her shoes off.

Before she returned to the conversation, the group was joined by Thomas Brown.

"Anything I can do in the morning, just let me know," he offered.

"Thank you," Violet said, seeming to be fully conscious again. "I think everything is under control. You have all done so much already."

Denis watched her closely. He loved the way her eyes seemed to dance when she was excited about something, and it was perfectly obvious to everyone that nothing excited her more than the school. Yes, you made a wise choice, he congratulated himself.

"You haven't answered my question yet," Arnold said.

"I'm sorry," Violet said. "I guess my mind was wandering. What did you want?"

"Denis has asked to escort you home," he said, that familiar twinkle present. "I said it was fine, as long as you agreed."

"I—I—I don't—think so—know..." she stammered.

"Good," Denis said, extending the crick in his elbow for her to hold. "Then it is settled."

"I said..." Violet tried to protest, but the words got lost somewhere between her voice box and her mouth.

"I know what you said," Denis said, "and I know what you meant."

"You are the most exasperating person I have ever met," Violet snapped. "You have no way of knowing what I meant." I'm not even sure I even know what I meant, she thought.

Arnold stopped them briefly. "Why don't you take the buggy?" he asked. "Mary Jane and I could use a little exercise. It is a beautiful night for a walk, and it isn't that far."

"Are you sure?" Denis asked.

Violet heard Led and Gentle Lamb snickering. She wondered what was so funny, but they were talking in Sioux, so she had no idea that they had both just described to each other what fun it would be to watch Denis hoisting Mistress Seymour up onto his horse, with her in her full array of petticoats and bare feet.

"Come along," Violet called out to Gentle Lamb. "Denis is going to take us home." She felt safe with her new little charge at her side.

"No," Arnold said firmly. "The children will go with us. You two youngsters go on."

Violet opened her mouth to protest, but before she could say anything Arnold reminded her, "Tomorrow you will begin your real work. You have already done a great deal. I dare say every child in Lake City is looking forward to the opening of school in the morning." He laughed. "Even Frank Patton."

Violet was tempted to ask who Frank Patton was. She had not heard anyone mention that name, and she knew she had not met a Patton family. She had made a careful notation of each family she had encountered, and the Pattons were nowhere on that list. She knew it all by heart.

Just like Denis's letter, she thought. She felt herself blush again, in spite of her recent efforts to try to control that action. It was such a stupid habit. If only she could break herself from doing it.

She reached up to her bosom, where she had carried the treasured letter for days. No, she reminded herself, it is not there. It ended up in shreds after your little episode in Lake Pepin. She had tried to reconstruct it, but it was hopeless. But, she didn't need it. Not really. She knew every single word it contained. It was easier to memorize than fine poetry.

She jumped, startled at the feeling of her own body. For the first time, she realized that she was still without her shoes or stockings. Her stockings were still there, tucked away neatly, where she had put them for safe keeping up on Sugar Loaf.

She felt Denis's eyes on her as they walked across the school yard to the Bowens' buggy. He was studying her body—all of it—intensely. She wanted to scream. She wanted to run and hide. She wanted to die of embarrassment.

"Is something wrong?" Denis asked. He hesitated momentarily before adding, "I did notice that you seemed..."—he cleared his throat before he continued— "exceptionally beautiful and well-endowed this evening."

Oh, dear! Violet thought. She had completely forgotten that her stockings were filling her chemise to new proportions. Had everyone noticed? How could she ever face the people of Lake City again?

Suddenly, as if overcome by some superhuman force, she pulled herself up to new heights for her five feet and two inches and took a deep breath. Let him think what he wanted to! Aunt Caroline, who was extremely well endowed, once told her, "Don't ever be ashamed of your body. It is what God gave you, so wear it proudly." She had then pushed her own breasts to their fullest and said loudly, "My dear, if you've got it, flaunt it!" Okay, so she was a Keith. And if Aunt Caroline could flaunt it, then so could she. Let him wonder. Maybe, if she was lucky, he would think she was wearing an extremely strong corset.

In a flash he had grasped her around the waist and was lifting her into the buggy. He paused, wishing he could keep her there forever. She felt incredibly delicious, like honey that melted in your mouth, or Mary Jane Bowen's homemade peach ice cream. His mouth watered just at the thought—of any of the three things his mind had conjured up.

Denis climbed in beside her. He handled the reins expertly through the open front of the buggy, not that he would need to, he thought. The Bowen's horses knew their way home, even in the middle of a raging blizzard, but he had no intention whatsoever of going directly home. The night was far too beautiful to waste, and so was the woman he was with.

Violet tipped her head upward and stared at the sky. There were just a few billowy clouds, and the full moon was reflecting in the inky black water in Lake Pepin. In the distance, the bluffs projected a dark silhouette, casting eerie feelings of the spirit world Uncle Lath had told her about the day Denis rescued Gentle Lamb.

Denis took note of every inch of her face, as if he was afraid he might one day forget it. Her nose, so tiny and upturned, reminded him of an elf. Her eyes, as green as the first leaves on the trees in the springtime, and the tiny freckles, which he could not see in the darkness but which he knew so well, were etched in his mind forever. She was, he knew, the most beautiful thing he had ever seen. Well, maybe except the water and the bluffs and the landscape Lake City had to offer. He had truly fallen in love with this place. How he hoped she had too. He didn't know what he would ever do if she decided to leave.

His whole body convulsed at the thoughts he was entertaining. He had hired a schoolmarm. He had no right to be thinking such things. He was her boss, nothing more, at least not yet.

"Are you okay?" Violet asked, surprised by his shaking.

"Yes," Denis answered. "I am wonderful."

Violet laughed. "You men! You are all so egotistical. Of course you think you are wonderful, but are you all right?"

"I'm that too," he said, laughing with her. How he loved the sound of her laughter. So pure. So trustworthy. So honest.

"The sky is gorgeous," Violet said, looking upward again.

"Yes, it is," Denis said. Suddenly, he tugged on the reins and ordered the team to stop.

"What are you doing?" Violet asked, edging away from his as far as she could.

"What I have wanted to do ever since I carried you out of the water," he said. He leaned over, ever so gently, and kissed her softly on the lips.

"Why, Denis McLeod! I never!" Violet shouted.

"Good," Denis said, laughing heartily. "I had hoped you would say that. You see, I wanted to be the first one to show you many of the marvels of Lake City." He ran his fingers over her face, tracing her cheekbones. "Including that one."

Violet knew she should protest, but she had to admit, this was what she had dreamed of night after night. And, she had to admit that it felt every bit as good as she had imagined it would.

"Just so it is proper," Denis said, looking longingly at her, "may I kiss you, Miss Seymour?"

Miss Seymour! The fact that he had not called her his mistress again seemed to make all the difference in the world, for some dumb reason. He would expect a mistress to kiss him. But Miss Seymour—he would have to ask her permission.

"I—I guess so," Violet said. She felt as shy as her name implied. "Shy Violet," she had been called as a child.

He kissed her again. This time it was not gentle, but passionate, desperate. She melted in his arms. She had heard her friends back in Illinois talking about how wonderful it felt to be in love, but she never imagined anything could feel this good. She didn't really know much about lovemaking, or loving, but nature seemed to take over. Before she knew what she was doing—or why—she found her bare toes running up and down along Denis's leg. She felt his body shudder in response. She could not know just how much response he was feeling—all the way from his toes to his groin and on up to his mouth, where his tongue sought entrance to her mouth. Oh, this is ecstasy! This is torture! This is heaven and hell at once, he thought.

~*~

As Denis directed the horse and buggy toward the barn, Gentle Lamb and Led came running up to them. Gentle Lamb pulled on Violet's hand, guiding her to a huge lilac bush in the Bowens' back yard. Led followed behind them, close on their heels.

"Where are you taking me?" Violet asked.

Gentle Lamb turned back to look at Led. He nodded, offering her the encouragement she needed.

"Sor-prize," Gentle Lamb said slowly.

When they got behind the lilac bush she could see Rose Petal crouching near the ground. In the moonlight she seemed to have a glow about her. Gentle Lamb grinned, then ran to her mother, hugging her tightly.

Violet knew immediately how much Rose Petal had risked to come here. Black Cloud had made it clear that no one—including Rose Petal—was to have any contact with Gentle Lamb. If he found her here she would surely be beaten, at the very least.

Denis stood in the background. He knew that Led could translate for the two women. He listened carefully as Rose Petal thanked Violet for caring for Gentle Lamb. Violet felt her heart nearly break for the woman who was entrusting a part of her very being to a near stranger.

Before long, both Violet and Rose Petal began to repeat words in each other's native tongue. Gentle Lamb beamed with pride as she said a word in Sioux, then put her hand on Violet's head and said, "Smart lady." She repeated it as she moved her hand to her mother's head.

"Smart lady?" Rose Petal asked.

Violet nodded.

"Two smart lady," Rose Petal said, pointing to herself and then to Violet.

"Yes, two smart ladies," Violet said. She sensed that she and Rose Petal could easily become good friends, yet she did not want to endanger her life by disobeying Black Cloud's orders.

Led explained to Violet that Rose Petal wanted Gentle Lamb to go to school with her.

"But Black Cloud?" Violet asked.

"She says he has already thrown Gentle Lamb to the wolves so it will not matter to him," Led said.

Violet quickly agreed. She would not only like to see Gentle Lamb learn English, but she would like her to teach the white children some Sioux words as well.

"Tell her she will go to school with me tomorrow morning," Violet said to Led.

"I told her that," Led said, "and I told her that I will accompany both of you in the morning."

"That is not necessary," Violet protested.

"Nonsense!" Led insisted. "It is most improper for two single ladies to be wandering the city alone."

Denis chuckled at Led's adult attitude. Perhaps the lad could teach him a bit about how to handle a woman.

Suddenly a roar echoed throughout the air. Violet grabbed hold of Rose Petal's arm.

"You must hide," Violet said, her voice trembling. "It must be Black Cloud."

Denis told Rose Petal and Gentle Lamb what Violet had said. They, joined by Led, broke into loud peals of laughter.

"He's dangerous," Violet insisted. "How can you laugh?"

"That's an elk," Led said. "Rose Petal is much safer from him than she would be from Black Cloud."

Violet was relieved that neither Rose Petal nor anyone else was in danger, but she wondered if she would ever get used to the strange sounds, people and practices of her new home.

"Who knew Paradise had such creatures?" she asked, making them laugh again.

CHAPTER 15

Violet lay flat on her back in the soft featherbed in her room at the Bowen house. Gentle Lamb, exhausted from a long day, was snoring peacefully.

She smiled in the darkness. Gentle Lamb had made such progress already. There were still words that she couldn't comprehend, but every day her vocabulary and understanding grew. She knew much of the credit belonged to Led, but she also felt that she had helped her a great deal.

A child's mind, she thought, is such a valuable commodity. Like a sponge, ready to absorb anything you pour into it.

She shivered as if a chill wind had blown through the room. She was overwhelmed with the sense of responsibility that awaited her. Was she really up to the challenge? It was a little late to question that now. In just a few hours she would be standing in front of the classroom at the new schoolhouse.

In spite of her misgivings, she realized that the townsfolk did trust her. They had proven that by their dedication to the new building. Even Uncle Alonzo had chipped in with a contribution. Aunt Caroline had told her that he had carefully built each desk. As she had thanked him, he carefully ran his fingers over the satiny smooth tops. "Can't be too careful where little ones is concerned," he said. "Wouldn't want a sliver on your first day of school."

Violet smiled again. "Uncle Lon," as they all called Alonzo, was the black sheep of the family. He didn't want to live with the rest of them. Forget the fact that he had settled across the lake in Wisconsin before the rest of the Keiths came to Lake City. By rights, she reasoned, that made the rest of them the renegades, not Uncle Lon. One thing was sure; he was the finest craftsman to be found in the area. The desks offered a mirror-like reflection, so well-done were they.

Children. With no warning, no explanation, Violet's mind filled with children. Her own children! She envisioned two boys and two girls. The girls looked exactly like her, but the boys were the spitting image of their father.

Violet sat bolt upright in bed, cold sweat pouring down her face. What on earth was wrong with her? She had no right to think such thoughts. Sure, Denis had kissed her, but that didn't mean she was about ready to bear his children. Besides, he was such an arrogant pomp sometimes that she wasn't sure she could tolerate some little versions of him.

Crazy ideas spun around in her mind faster than a whirling dervish. "Get ahold of yourself!" she silently ordered. "You have to get some sleep. Tomorrow is a big day, and you can't afford to let your mind wander like this. What would the children think?"

~*~

Finally, after a few more hours of fitful sleep, Violet awakened to the first warm rays of the morning sun. She quickly jumped up and ran to the window, pulling the rope to raise the shade. As if offering a promise, the bluffs at Sugar Loaf seemed to shine more brightly than ever. The multi-colored sand appeared to dance playfully in the reflection on the water. Now that she had actually been there, it was even more fascinating than before. What kind of magic did it hold? Denis had warned her of its power and mysticism, but she was not prepared for the fullness of its effects.

What would have happened if Denis had come to her up on the bluffs? The answer echoed so loudly in her head that she turned around to look for a person who might have spoken. Assured that she was alone, she looked back at Sugar Loaf. No, she would never allow him to do that to her. Not until they were married, she told herself, and Denis McLeod just didn't seem like the marrying type.

Her muscles tightened, recalling the feelings she had experienced the night before when Denis kissed her. She had never known anything that created such strong emotions. From the top of her head to the ends of her toes... She laughed, remembering that she had been barefoot for the entire time of the welcoming party. She hoped no one had noticed. Even more, she hoped no one had noticed that her figure, which was quite well enough endowed under normal circumstances, was a bit more abundant than normal.

She thought about Mrs. Bowen's Sears & Roebuck catalog the two of them had studied so many times, dreaming of wearing such fine garments here in this "heathen land," as Mrs. Bowen was prone to call it. They had discussed such womanly things as the "falsies" the catalog offered "to make a fine and lasting impression on the opposite sex; to make the female more appealing." It was, they both agreed, a most disgusting ploy.

"If the good Lord intended us all to look like Maude Hampsten," Mrs. Bowen had remarked, "he would have endowed us all equally."

Violet cringed at the thought that some of the people might have thought that she would resort to such a means to impress the men in the community. What in the world had made her stuff her stockings in there? She could just as easily have stuck them inside her bloomers. The next time...

"I'm ready," Gentle Lamb said, jumping out of bed like a flash of lightening. "Today is school, yes?" she asked.

"Yes," Violet said, motioning for Gentle Lamb to join her at the window. "It is so pretty," she said, pointing to Sugar Loaf.

"Pretty, like Spring Flower," Gentle Lamb said, nuzzling up tightly against her newly adopted mother.

"You are so good for my ego," Violet said, running her fingers through the child's long, coarse black hair.

"He go where?" Gentle Lamb asked, obviously confused by the new word Violet had used.

"Not he go," Violet explained, "but ego. That is the part of you that..." She paused, trying to figure out the best way to explain the term to Gentle Lamb. "The part of you that makes you like yourself."

Gentle Lamb grinned up at her. "Do you like you?" she asked.

"Yes," Violet admitted, "at least most of the time I do. It is a good thing to like yourself. If you do not like yourself, it is very hard to like other people."

"Then I like me too," Gentle Lamb said proudly, "because I like you. And I like Led. If I like them, then I have to like me too."

"I think you have every reason in the universe to like yourself," Violet said. "You are a very pretty little girl and you are very smart. I am proud of you."

"The eagle is proud," Gentle Lamb said. "Denis told me so. If Denis says so, then I know it is true." She fondled the plume on her medicine wheel.

Violet jumped at the idea that Gentle Lamb swallowed everything Denis said as absolute truth. If he really was a man of his word, had he meant it when he kissed her? The thought thrilled her—and frightened her at the same time.

"Breakfast is ready," Mrs. Bowen called upstairs to them.

"We must hurry to get dressed," Violet said. She watched as Gentle Lamb scurried into her very best suede leather dress. It was all adorned with hand beading and porcupine quills her mother had done before Little Flower—went away—Violet thought. She hated death! It was so—final! She was so glad Rose Petal had come to see them last night.

Violet washed up, shivering at the coolness of the water which had stood in the ewer over night. She put on her best skirt and blouse, which she had carefully ironed the night before and hung up to keep it fresh and neat for the big day.

"You look like a beautiful portrait," the well-known voice of Denis McLeod said.

His presence was startling—unsettling—to say the least. He had no right being here this early in the morning. What if she had just pulled on her robe and come down for breakfast, as she had done some mornings? What a mortifying thought!

"What's the matter?" he asked, winking at Arnold. "I thought, since I am responsible for your being here and the whole school shindig, that it was only fitting that I escort you to the school for your first day."

"I thank you for your offer," Violet said, "but I know the way quite well." Truth of the matter was, she admitted to herself, she didn't want the whole town making her the topic of the daily gossip, especially not if anyone had happened to see them last night.

"I take her to school," Gentle Lamb said. "I know way well."

"I'm sure you do," Denis said, glaring at Violet. So she was going to assert her independence anyway. He had warned her about allowing the Indians into the school. She was headed for trouble, sure as anything, but if he said anything now he knew he would offend Gentle Lamb, and he didn't want to do that, either. Try as he might, he couldn't help the love and attraction he felt for her. For both of them. Just a few weeks ago he had had no woman in his life—not even a thought of one—and now he had two, and he didn't really know what to do with either one of them.

"I will be glad to accompany her," Led said, acting far too grown up for his six years. "I already told her so."

Denis realized that perhaps that would be the best way to handle it.

"If you are sure," he told Led. "If anything happens to her, I'll hold you responsible."

"Mr. McLeod!" Mrs. Bowen shouted. "How dare you threaten a mere child?"

"I'm sorry, ma'am," Denis said. "I didn't mean anything by it. I know Led is as capable as any of the men in town. Perhaps more so."

"And don't you forget it!" Mrs. Bowen said. "Now, won't you join us for some coffee, oatmeal and fresh biscuits? I just took them out of the oven."

"I'd love to," Denis said, sitting down at the table with them.

His knee twitched as he remembered the kiss he and Violet had shared last night. He couldn't seem to take his eyes off her. So she wanted to be independent; fine, but he would follow along behind just to be sure.

"Do you suppose you could give me a hand?" Arnold asked Denis. "I have to get Maude Hampsten's house ready to move, and it's looking like a mighty big job."

"Sure," Denis said, wishing he could think of a logical reason why he couldn't. Well, it looked like he was going to have to trust Led with his—with the school mistress after all. But that didn't mean he had to like it.

CHAPTER 16

Violet, Led and Gentle Lamb walked down the winding trail through Lake City on their way to the new school. They chattered gaily, with Gentle Lamb being so excited she frequently relapsed into her native Sioux.

"You have to talk English," Led cautioned her. "If you don't, the other children will tease you."

"I speak only English from now forward," she said, grinning at her grasp of the strange language.

Violet smiled proudly at her. "You have learned so quickly," she said. "You are a very bright little girl."

"The sun is bright," Gentle Lamb said. The three of them were holding hands, with Violet in the middle, and swinging them back and forth as they walked. Gentle Lamb held her free arm up in front of her and studied it carefully. "It does not look bright to me."

Violet and Led laughed. "Okay," Violet said. "Let me say that again. You are a very smart little girl."

"I want to learn good in school," Gentle Lamb said. "Then the people will not make me stay away."

Violet felt her stomach churn. She had completely forgotten about Denis's warning not to get the Indian children involved. Was that why he had wanted to accompany her to school the first day? Was she headed for trouble?

She wished with all her heart that he was walking along beside her. Her knees felt weak. Perhaps, if no one said anything about Gentle Lamb...

"Who are you trying to fool?" she asked herself. As soon as she spoke her name, the secret would be out. Even before that they would know. One look at her shiny black braids and her beaded suede dress would tell them without a single word being spoken.

"Let's skip," Led suggested. Without thinking about the image a teacher should portray, Violet joined with them. She waved at the people she passed, inviting them to bring their children so they wouldn't be late on the first day of classes.

One by one the mothers and their children joined behind them until they had a procession the likes of which Lake City had never seen.

"I knew it!" Led said disgustedly as they got to the school yard. Willie Webster was already there, waiting to welcome them. "Now he will get to ring the bell."

"I told you you could ring it," Violet reminded him. "I always keep my promises. Go on inside and ring it."

Led rushed ahead, and soon the bell was pealing throughout the whole town. Violet beamed at the announcement, although it was completely unnecessary. She was sure everyone who had any reason to be there was already assembled. Everybody except Denis McLeod. It wasn't fair. After all, she had to admit that this was really his school. Without him, there wouldn't be any school.

~*~

Arnold Bowen and Denis rode their horses out towards the Rahilly house. Arnold noticed that Denis, who was usually quite talkative, was nearly silent today. He had sensed that Violet wanted to handle the school challenge alone. She had worked so hard in the short time she had been there to get everything ready, he felt that was the least she deserved.

Now, watching Denis mope along, he knew he had made a mistake.

"You might as well go chase after her," Arnold said.

"After who?" Denis asked, as if he didn't know.

"The Queen of England," Arnold said, teasing his young friend. "Who do you think?"

"Oh, did you mean Mistress Seymour?"

"Yes," Arnold said, laughing at how nervous Denis seemed suddenly, "but I should think, after the way you have been ogling her ever since she arrived, that you might start calling her Violet."

Now it was Denis's turn to laugh. "A fine one you are to talk! How many times have I heard you call your wife Mrs. Bowen?"

"That is quite different," Arnold insisted. "By rights she should be addressed as 'Lady.' She is, you know, almost royalty, being descended from Lord Stirling and all. The only thing that woman has ever done wrong in her life was marry a poor nobody."

"Don't sell yourself short," Denis said. "She nearly worships the ground you walk on."

"And I will never know why, if I live to be a hundred and two," Arnold said, "but I thank the good Lord above every day of my life that she loves me."

Denis smiled warmly at Arnold. Never before had he discussed such things with another man. His lips burned as he felt the kiss he and Violet had shared. Was this the love the poets spoke about? Or was it just a physical attraction? When he was with her, he felt like his whole body was on fire. When he was away from her, his body ached, just to touch her elbow. Or to see her smile. Or watch her little button nose quiver when she laughed. Or see the way her freckles became a deeper, darker hue when she blushed.

"Go on," Arnold ordered. "You won't be any good to me anyway. Just be careful."

Denis turned back towards town and jabbed his heels into the horse's side. As he rode away he heard Arnold call out to him, "Maybe you shouldn't let her know you are there."

Denis shook his head. He had never known just how much of a sly character Arnold Bowen was. He wondered if Mary Jane Bowen realized it. Yes, he thought, and she is probably equal to his pranks any day of the year.

Nearing the school grounds, Denis could see that the children were all inside and the classes were already in session. He wanted to see what was going on, but he didn't want to alert Violet of his presence. After all, Arnold had said...

He jumped off his horse and secured it to a tree. He crept along behind the bushes, careful to keep himself well out of view. He was almost close enough to see through the sparkling glass window from Chicago when...

"Whatcha doin' there, Denis?" a voice called out, loud enough to wake the dead. "If you want to go to school, why don'tcha go on in? I s'pects Miss Seymour, she'd be mighty glad to see you."

Violet walked over to the window when she heard the commotion. She was just in time to see Denis and Frank Patton get sprayed by a passing skunk.

"You...you damned rat!" Denis shouted. "I always knew you were a real stinker, but this! Did you have to involve me in your stupid pranks?"

Denis's face was red with rage. He didn't dare look towards the window. He was certain by now that not only Violet, but the entire school knew of his plight.

"You think I planned this?" Frank Patton asked. "Believe me, if I had I wouldn't have gotten in the line of fire." Unexplainably, Frank was rolling around on the ground laughing. No one else would have thought this was the least bit amusing, but this was not just anyone. This was Frank Patton. And everybody in Lake City knew there was nobody like Frank Patton.

Violet tried to shoo the children back to their desks, but they were all too involved by now to do anything but watch. She bit her upper lip. She wanted so badly to laugh. She had heard of Frank Patton, and although she had never met him, instinct told her that she was seeing him now, and even though he was strange, he had every right to be bowled over with laughter. Yes, this was by far funnier than the day she fell in the lake.

When the children were finally in their proper desks, Violet tried to conduct the class again. She carefully continued writing the letters on the slate Alonzo had attached to the wall. She got as far as "t" when she saw out of the corner of her eye that Frank and Denis were leaving. Her glance was just in time to catch a rabbit hopping out of their path as fast as it could. Even the bunny was smart enough to stay out of the way of a skunk—or its victims, she thought.

"Mistress Seymour," little Penelope Griffin said, breaking Violet's concentration on the outsiders, "I'm stuck."

Violet looked at the girl and realized that she was indeed stuck. She was trying to pry her way out of the space which was allotted for sitting between the desk top and the seat. Uncle Lon had done well in designing the desks different sizes, and had placed them in their proper areas for the various grades. Since there was only one room to the schoolhouse, Violet had divided the "grades" by the sizes of the desks. Then she divided the "grades" by the ages of each child. Not that it made much difference, she knew. Hardly any of them knew even the basics of the abc's or the 1-2-3's, but the youngest children were placed in the first grade and the oldest children were placed in the fifth grade. That way, she reasoned, she would have at least four years to get even the oldest students out of grammar school. Little Penelope Griffin was only six years old, which meant that she was in the first grade, but she was obviously too plump for the first-grade desks. She was definitely stuck!

Violet went to help her. She pulled on her from one side, then the other. Nothing seemed to work. She wondered if she should send for Uncle Lon to come and cut her free. It would be such a waste of a good desk. He might even refuse to do it, but she couldn't leave Penelope there for the rest of her life.

"Willie," she said to Willie Webster, "could you please come help me?" She had picked Willie, not because he was the smartest boy there, but because he was the biggest.

Willie came over to Penelope and began pulling on one hand while Violet pulled on the other. It didn't help. Penelope didn't budge.

"Here," little Maggie Brown said, holding a slice of bread out to Violet. "Maybe this will help."

By this time every child there was snickering, except Penelope. She had burst into tears, which certainly wasn't helping matters any.

Violet tried to comfort Penelope, and at the same time control the other children. This was as humiliating for Penelope as falling in the lake had been for her, or getting sprayed by a polecat was for Denis.

"Penelope is already stuck," Violet said. "Giving her too much to eat is what got her into this predicament in the first place. I don't see how feeding her bread and butter is going to do any good."

"No," Maggie said. "You don't feed it to her. You smear it all over her."

Violet tried to envision Penelope going home to her mother with butter smeared all over her from head to toe. She knew, at that very moment, that her career as a teacher was over. She was a failure, unless she could figure some other way out.

"Don't you see?" Maggie asked. "I saw Papa grease up a pig one time when it got stuck in the slats of the fence. If it worked with a pig, it should work with Penelope too."

Poor Penelope began wailing even louder. "Maggie called me a pig!" she bellowed.

"Did not," Maggie insisted.

"Did so," Penelope yelled back.

"Did not," Maggie repeated.

"Children!" Violet said sternly. "Fighting or calling names is not going to help anyone. You do have a point, Maggie. Perhaps it is worth a try."

"Why don't we put the butter on the desk instead of on Penelope?" Led asked.

Violet smiled. She wondered if Led, as young as he was, would always be there to rescue her. She wondered why she always seemed to need rescuing. Was it a curse, or just dumb luck?

"That is a good idea," Violet said, taking the slice of bread from Maggie and rubbing it on the wood at the bottom of the desk top. She managed to wrench her fingers, squeezed as they were, between Penelope's round tummy and the desk.

"Okay," she said to Willie, "let's try it again."

They both pulled, and with one loud slurp sound Penelope slid out quite nicely.

"Now don't sit back in there," Violet ordered. The children were still snickering at the whole affair. "I think we have a solution. Can you fit into a third grade desk?" She eyed the desk where Josie Webster was sitting. "Josie, would you mind?" she asked, and Josie was soon on her feet, waiting to see if Violet's plan would work.

Penelope slid in and out several times with no trouble at all.

"Then that is solved," Violet said. "Penelope, you are now in the third grade and Josie, while you are small enough to fit into the first-grade desk, you are still in third grade, but you will have to sit in that desk until we can see if Uncle Lon will make a new desk for you."

"Yes, ma'am," Josie said shyly, taking her place amongst the first graders.

I am going to have to take extra time with Josie, Violet thought. She seems so withdrawn. I wonder...

Her thought was interrupted by the whinnying of a horse. She went to the door and saw Denis's mare standing just outside the door. Her reins were hanging loose, broken by the efforts it had taken to free it from the tree where Denis had tied it. In his hurry to get away from the scene of the crime, which had been committed by a poor defenseless skunk, Denis had apparently not even thought about the horse. All he wanted to do was to get away from the site, from his humiliation, and get the problem rectified.

"Led," Violet asked, "would you please tie the horse to the post outside?"

Led went obediently and did as she asked.

Violet returned to the lessons, which they pursued until she looked at the big old clock on the wall. It was just a few minutes before the noon hour.

"We will break for lunch," Violet said. "You will have one hour to eat your lunch and play outside. At one o'clock the bell will ring. You must then all line up by the door to return for the afternoon classes."

~*~

Denis sat in the wash tub in Mrs. Bowen's kitchen. His skin was red from the tomato juice she had poured into the tub. He was still rubbing, scrubbing, trying to rid himself of his stench.

"How's it coming?" Mrs. Bowen called from the parlor. "I'm going to have to get the bread on baking pretty soon."

"I'm almost finished," Denis called back to her. "I think it worked. Now I just have to figure out how to get the tomato juice off."

Mrs. Bowen laughed. She and Denis had formed a close friendship right from the beginning. After all, they were both Scots. That in itself was nearly enough to make them kinfolk, but above that, they seemed to have a silent, unspoken understanding of each other, even now.

"I'll fetch a bucket of water from the pump," she said, "but I'll have to come into the kitchen to pour it on you. You'll have to dump the tub yourself. Just toss it out the back door." She gave a sinister smirk as she added, "I promise I won't peek."

Denis stood up in the tub. He set the towel on the floor, then dried his feet and legs off, leaving red stains on it. He picked up the tub and, naked as a jaybird, opened the back door and dumped the tomato juice off to the side of the steps.

"I sure am glad Violet isn't here to see this," he mumbled to himself.

CHAPTER 17

"You go on ahead," Violet told Led and Gentle Lamb. "I have some things to get ready for tomorrow morning."

"Are you sure?" Led asked. His father had never allowed his mother to wander around town without an escort. He felt uneasy leaving her alone.

"I'll be just fine," Violet assured him. "Tell your mother I won't be long."

Obediently, the two children skipped down the trail to the Bowen house, talking non-stop about the thrill of their first day of school.

"Where is Mistress Seymour?" Mrs. Bowen asked as they came in.

"She said she'll be home soon," Led explained. "She had some things to do at school."

Denis, who was still there, in spite of the fact that he knew he should have gone off to help Uncle Lath on the ferry, hurried to pull his hat on and head out the door. He was still nervous about the fact that Gentle Lamb had gone to school. Maybe he was being paranoid, but it spelled trouble to him. He really hoped he was wrong. He'd had about all the trouble he could tolerate for one day. With a little bit of luck, he hoped she hadn't seen his encounter with the enemy, but he knew that was pretty unlikely.

Violet was just pulling the door shut as he arrived. She bent over to pick up the stack of books she was taking home to prepare the next day's lessons. She was so intent on her thoughts that she didn't see Denis standing there, watching her every move.

Oblivious to everything, she began to walk, looking down as she went to make sure she didn't trip and fall on the rough sod the men had put in place in the yard. She nearly ran into him before he said, "May I carry your books home from school, ma'am?"

Violet jumped, startled by his voice, causing not only her books to drop to the ground, but her papers to scatter in every direction. Denis hurried to scamper after them, his arms flailing every which way in the wind to keep them from getting lost.

"What would you ever do without me?" he asked when he had retrieved them all. She hated it when he got that sinister grin on his face. She hated it when he was right. Worst of all, she hated admitting she really did need him, far more than she was willing to admit—to herself, and certainly to him.

"I guess I'd just have to fight all the polecats by myself," she said, hoping she could embarrass him as much as he did her. Seeing his face lower, staring at the ground nervously, she knew it had worked.

"You saw?" he asked stupidly. Of course she had seen him. No doubt the whole school had seen him. He and Frank weren't exactly quiet out there in the bushes.

She didn't say a word, just nodded her head, then laughed—long and hard.

Denis wanted to crawl under a rock someplace. He wished he could make himself invisible. He wondered if the tomato juice had really worked its wonders, as Mrs. Bowen had promised it would, or if he still bore the remains of the nasty varmint.

"I'm sorry," Violet managed to say through the guffaws. "It's just that—it was so funny!"

"As funny as you in the drink?" he asked, hoping that the reminder of her own escapade would cause her to forget his plight.

"At least ten times funnier," she said, biting her lip to try to keep from laughing any more. She knew that his pride was hurt far more than his skin, which seemed none the worse for wear, she had to admit.

Suddenly she stretched up on her tiptoes and kissed him.

"What was that for?" he asked.

"Do I need a reason?" Violet teased. "I thought, after last night…"

"Oh, no," Denis said, trying to take her in his arms but stopped by the load of books he had. "You have my permission to do that any time you want."

"Humph!" Violet snorted. "I don't need your permission to do anything. In case you haven't noticed, I'm a big girl now."

"Believe me," Denis said, grinning at her, "I've definitely noticed." He chuckled as he added, "Of course you don't seem quite as big today as you did last night."

Violet turned crimson. He was staring right at her bosom. Those fool stockings! Why on earth had she put them there? And even worse, why hadn't she bothered to take them out?

"Cat got your tongue?" he joked.

"No," she said, sticking it out at him to prove her point was valid. "There, see? It's still here."

"Good," he said, feeling his flesh boil as he thought of how it would feel to kiss her like he really longed to do, with his lips tight against hers, and his tongue probing deep into her mouth, finding pleasure in the mingling of the two of them.

He leaned forward and kissed her in return. It was a long, slow, passionate kiss. He felt his body respond in ways which he could not control. He longed to caress her gently, to make love to her, to claim her as his own—not just as his schoolmarm, but as his lover. It was a good thing his hands were full.

Violet quickly pulled away from him.

"This is crazy!" she said. "Here we are in broad daylight in the middle of the schoolyard making out like a couple of love-starved puppies."

"So?" Denis asked. "It seems to me we are just doing what comes naturally."

"So was the skunk," Violet said, bringing up the dreaded subject again, "and look at the trouble that caused."

"Ouch!" Denis said, wounded by her barbed remarks. "Well, as we began this conversation, may I carry your books home for you, Mistress Seymour, as long as I have them anyway?"

"Yes, sir," Violet said. "If you behave like a gentleman."

"Always," Denis said, bowing deeply to her. "Shall we?" He extended his arm for her to take ahold of. Violet began walking, quickly, a couple of steps ahead of him, with her hands swinging freely at her side.

"So are you going to tell me your secret?" she asked as they walked.

"Secret?" Denis asked, not knowing what she meant.

"Yes," she replied. "How did you get rid of the smell? It must have been terrible."

"I'll never tell," he said, wondering if she was trying to prepare herself in case she ever needed the same treatment.

As they approached the Bowen house, Led and Gentle Lamb were out in the back yard, digging a hole.

"What are you doing?" Violet called out to them.

"Burying these!" Led called back as he held up Denis's clothes on a stick. "They'll never be fit for man or beast again."

"You stink!" Gentle Lamb said, pleased that she had learned a new word. "Peee-ew!"

Violet was chuckling again, trying not to let Denis see her. She knew how humiliated he must be, but after the way he rubbed her nose in her mishap when she arrived, she really couldn't feel too sorry for him. He only got what was coming to him.

~*~

"We really have to do something," Mrs. Webster said to Mrs. Merrill. "As if it isn't bad enough having Frank Patton trying to get into school—at his age, yet! But she actually brought that redskin along with her. It's one thing to try to rescue the little thing. That's fine. But to take her to school! Hasn't anybody told her you can't educate them? We've got to stop her."

"Come on," Mrs. Merrill said. "Time's a wastin'." They headed down the street, their steps filled with determination. Black Cloud watched from a distance as they began knocking on the first door they came to. He knew there was going to be trouble. He could feel it in the wind.

CHAPTER 18

There was not one second's lull in the conversation at the Bowens' in the afternoon once Violet arrived. She and Denis went into the kitchen, where Mrs. Bowen was listening to Led and Gentle Lamb tell all about the events of the day. One would start a sentence and the other, as if pre-programmed, would finish it. She was amazed at how fast Gentle Lamb was learning English. When she was stumped by a word, Led would give the Sioux word to her, followed by the English word. She never seemed to forget it once she had repeated it aloud.

Violet noticed that neither of them mentioned the incident with Denis and the skunk. She wondered if Denis had confronted them on their way home from school and warned them about bringing the matter up. It would be just like him, she thought. So arrogant!

She put her hand over her mouth, hoping they wouldn't notice that she was laughing. She couldn't help herself. Soon she was laughing louder, then louder, until tears ran down her cheeks.

"Something funny?" Denis asked. "Apparently we all missed it."

"Nothing," she said, rubbing her eyes with the back of her hand.

"Sounds frightfully amusing to me," Mrs. Bowen said, trying to keep a straight face. She could just about imagine what she was thinking. She knew everybody in the school must have been a witness to the skunk episode. Her stomach ached from trying to hold her own glee inside. "I could really use a good laugh."

"I think she is laughing at Arms-of-Steel," Gentle Lamb said, gleams dancing about in her own eyes. "He—he—he was very funny."

She joined Violet in the laughter. Soon the four of them were hysterical.

Denis glared at Violet. He certainly didn't think it was as funny as all that. The nerve of the woman! He didn't laugh at her when she fell in the lake. Well, he hadn't laughed too hard. Well, he didn't laugh too many times. Or too long.

Suddenly, he saw the same funny picture half the town—at least the younger half—saw when they looked out the window. He had to admit, if it had happened to somebody else, anybody else, he would have found it as entertaining as they did. In spite of his most noble efforts, he began to laugh with them. Funny, he thought, how contagious good laughter can be. He wondered if anybody had ever been successful in not laughing when everyone around them was in stitches.

Arnold Bowen walked in the back door. The somber look on his face changed the mood instantly.

"What's the matter?" Mrs. Bowen asked, her expression changing from amusement to worry. She knew her husband all too well. Something was definitely wrong.

"There's trouble afoot," Arnold said. "Bad trouble."

"What is it?" Mrs. Bowen asked.

"Led, will you and Gentle Lamb please go outside and play?"

"Why, Father?" Led asked. If there was something wrong, he had a right to know too. Even if he was only six years old, he was a big six years old.

"I was out at the Rahilly house all day," he explained. "I saw Laura Merrill and Catherine Webster heading for town in the carriage like a bat out of hell. I still had work to do, but I had to let it be for a bit."

They all sat, wondering what the two women were up to. Violet didn't know the women very well yet, but she had heard that they were the town troublemakers. What had she done wrong? And how could she do anything that terrible on just the first day of school?

"Well," Arnold continued, "I followed them. They went from one door to the next, telling them that Mistress Seymore had allowed a redskin in at the school. Why, to listen to the two of them tell it, you'd think somebody had put poison in the water in the pump out back."

"Did they say what they were planning to do about it?" Denis asked.

"They've got Thomas Brown talked into calling a town meeting tonight." He hesitated. "I don't suppose they came here to invite us. I imagine they figure we're the enemy, since Gentle Lamb is living here."

"Nobody's come," Mrs. Bowen said.

"Well, I don't know about the rest of you," Denis said, standing up and fidgeting from one foot to the other, "but I'm going, invited or not."

"I'm with you," Arnold said. "Have you got supper on? We'd better eat early, just so we can be sure to get there on time."

"What time is the meeting?" Mrs. Bowen asked.

"Seven o'clock," Arnold answered, "but we've got chores to do before we go."

"I'm going too," Violet announced.

"Do you think that is a good idea?" Denis asked. "You're liable to be crucified."

Violet looked horrified. "They wouldn't really, would they?"

"I didn't mean literally," Denis said. "It is just that they will tear you up one side and down the other. Are you sure you are up to it?"

"I can handle it fine," Violet snapped. "I don't need you watching over my every move."

"Too bad," Denis said, grinning at her. "I was going to offer to hold your hand."

Violet blushed. He would like to do more than that. He would like to take her in his arms right now and tell her that everything was going to be okay. To tell her that he would take care of her, would protect her, no matter what happened.

"I'll stay here with Led and Gentle Lamb," Mrs. Bowen said. "But I'll be thinking about you."

"Thank you," Violet said. Sensing Mrs. Bowen's nervousness about her going, she added, "I'll be careful."

"Thank you," Mrs. Bowen said softly, her eyes filled with concern for her new boarder. She was surprised to realize that this young woman had come to mean so much to her in such a short time. She had always remained somewhat aloof from the other women in the community. The last time she had had a real close friend, Arnold had decided to up and move west. She had vowed then and there that she would never again become so attached to anyone, except her own family, of course. Now she had done it all over again. And this time it smelled of danger.

Denis gladly accepted the offer to eat with them. He didn't want to let Violet out of his sight, not even for a minute. She might need him.

Who was he trying to kid? He knew the real truth of the matter was that he needed her—for the school, naturally. He had started this whole school business when he wrote to King, enlisting his help in finding a schoolmarm. Now that he had her, what was he going to do with her? He knew the simple solution to the problem: keep Gentle Lamb out of the school.

His thoughts turned to the day he had rescued the child. He still hated the Indians with a passion, for what they had done to... No, he didn't want to go back down that path. He had relived the incident too many times. Still, he had to admit that it wasn't the fault of some mere child. She was as innocent as—as he was—for what had happened.

He debated about asking Violet to leave Gentle Lamb with Mrs. Bowen during the day. He knew she wouldn't mind. He also knew, as stubborn as the woman was, she would never agree to such a demand. No, there had to be another way, and he supposed it was up to him to find it, since he was responsible for the new school's mere existence.

Suddenly an idea struck him. What if she taught the regular children during the day, then at night held a short session for the Indian children? They would need someplace for them to go, but maybe Mrs. Bowen...

He couldn't ask her to do that. She had already been so good to Violet, allowing her to keep Gentle Lamb there with her. She had to know the people in town were all talking about it. Why else did she think so many of them went across the street when they saw her coming? They didn't want to be seen associating with an "Indian lover."

"I can't stop Gentle Lamb from attending school," Violet said, startling Denis. Had he only thought such things, or had he actually voiced them unknowingly?

"You certainly can't!" Arnold said. "And you shouldn't have to. She has the same rights as any other child in town."

"Rights?" Denis asked. He had never before thought about the matter, but he knew the Indians had no rights. They didn't even have a right to the land they had once called their own. Treaties had been made, and broken, by the government, proving that they had no rights, not even to a decent education.

"We'd better get going," Arnold said as he took the last sip of his tea. Turning to Violet he asked, "Are you sure you want to do this? We—Denis and I—we'll be glad to speak on your behalf. I think we both know how you feel."

"I can't trust him to do that," Violet insisted. "I know how he feels about the Indians."

"But Gentle Lamb is different," Denis argued. "I would fight for her to be able to attend."

"Don't you see?" Violet asked, her eyes heated from such prejudice. "This isn't just about Gentle Lamb. What if some of the other children want to come? Do we allow Gentle Lamb to go just because she is living in a white man's house but stop the other children from learning? No, if Gentle Lamb goes, they all go."

"Very well," Arnold said. "If there is anyone who can convince them, I guess it is you." He winked at Mrs. Bowen. "You know, she would make a Bowen proud. She's a woman who's as stubborn as all outdoors when she believes in something, just like my mother was."

"Right," Mrs. Bowen grumbled. "Any woman who is fool enough to marry a Bowen has to be stubborn. How else do you think we would survive?"

Violet smiled at the way the two of them, so obviously in love, exchanged playful verbal darts back and forth. There might not be any other Bowen men available in Lake City, but there was at least one eligible bachelor who was just as bullheaded as a Bowen, and she was looking right at him.

CHAPTER 19

Arnold Bowen, Denis and Violet rode up to the school house in the Bowen carriage. They all glanced around nervously, surveying the situation.

"Looks like we're the first ones here," Mr. Bowen said. "You two go on inside and I'll take the carriage around back. It'd probably be best if we took them by surprise."

"Maybe we should wait out back too," Violet said.

"I'm not putting you out behind some building like a common criminal," Denis snapped. "You didn't do anything wrong."

Violet almost asked if he was sure of that. She did know how he felt about the Indians. She remained silent, smiling to herself. Even Denis had to admit that Gentle Lamb had won his heart. Whatever his reasons for hating the redskins, they weren't good enough to stand between him and the tiny girl he had so bravely rescued.

Such a hero, Violet thought. First he rescues me from the lake, then he rescues Gentle Lamb. She wondered who would be next, or how many there had been before the two of them.

As she sat at her desk, she twisted her fingers nervously in and around each other. Her mind wandered back over the past weeks. The time had gone so quickly, yet it seemed, as she reflected, that she had been a part of Lake City forever. She did love it here. There was something wonderfully enchanting about just being here. She admitted, reluctantly, that she owed Denis MacLeod a great deal. To have such an offer just as she finished her training in normal school was beyond belief. A new school! To be the one to break ground in a new town was a dream come true.

"So what have you done with that dream?" she silently asked herself. "You have caused a rift in the village itself, all because of some Indians."

She looked at Denis, who was busily chatting with Arnold Bowen about their dilemma. He was such a complex individual. He claimed to hate the Indians, and most of the time he acted like he really did, yet he was as kind and compassionate to Gentle Lamb as anyone could ever hope. If he didn't have a soft spot in his heart for them, why did they select him to negotiate with Black Cloud? It appeared that they did respect him. Will the real Denis MacLeod please stand up? she thought, remembering a childhood game they used to play.

She blushed uncontrollably as she recalled their kiss the night before. It was so delightfully fulfilling she wished she could do it again, right here—right now.

"Don't you think that is best?" Arnold Bowen was asking her when she snapped back to the present.

"I'm sorry," she said. "I guess my mind was wandering. What did you say?"

"Never mind," Arnold said, seeing several people pull up outside the schoolhouse. "There's no time to worry about it now."

Thomas Brown, Uncle Lon, Uncle Lath and Captain Fuller were the first ones there. Good, Violet thought, I am sure they will be on my side.

"You will stand up for what's right, Thomas?" Arnold asked.

"I am afraid I cannot take either side," he said. "As the mayor, it is my job to referee. I must let the people decide what they want."

"Yellow-belly!" Denis mumbled, just loud enough to be heard.

Before Thomas Brown could call the meeting to order, Kate Webster walked in and began to speak.

"I'll not have my children mingling with the likes of those lowlifes!" she said, tapping her foot angrily as she spoke. "There may be a place in God's creation for them, but for the life of me I don't know where it is. One thing is certain; it's not with the likes of our own children."

"Here! Here!" Cries of agreement echoed from around the room.

Violet's head began to reel. She had met all these people, yet tonight they seemed like total strangers. Try as she might, she could hardly distinguish one face from another.

"Order!" Thomas Brown said, banging his gavel on Violet's brand new desk. Uncle Lon Keith gritted his teeth, hoping he hadn't put a dent in it already.

Kate Webster remained standing.

"Kate," the mayor said, "please take your seat. You may speak when you are addressed properly."

A snicker went through the room. No one could ever remember anyone telling a Webster to be quiet. No, words were what the Websters excelled in, and Kate, who was merely married to a Webster, let more than her share of them fly at every given opportunity.

"Perhaps we should hold a trial of the new schoolmarm," someone suggested. "If over two-thirds of us finds her guilty of messin' with the school system, then we can send her back to where she came from."

"Now just a minute!" Arnold Bowen said. "You were all anxious to have a school for your young ones. Suppose there are some redskins attending. So what? Why, you all know that my wife—Mary Jane Alexander, Lady Stirling by all rights—has taken the child in question into our own home."

"Shame on you!" Laura Merrill said.

"There's no shame in helping your neighbor," Arnold said. "If there is any shame, it is with all of you. Why, Jesus Himself taught us that we should help one another. And you, Laura Merrill, the superintendent of the Sunday School! Why, you should be ashamed of yourself."

Laura Merrill hung her head. She knew he was right. How could she ever face the children in Sunday School if she was a hypocrite?

"I say we let the girl stay," she said softly.

"Never!" Kate Webster insisted. "I'll withdraw Willie and Josie first, as much as they should have a good education."

"You'd let them do without no learnin' just 'cuz some little girl don't look the same?" came a voice from the back of the room.

They all turned to see who was speaking. To Violet's surprise, it was Frank Patton.

"You all know that I came here today intendin' to make trouble," he said. "Well, I met trouble on the way."

They all laughed. Word had quickly spread across town about Frank and Denis's encounter earlier in the day. What did such a scoundrel as Frank Patton know about school?

"Even after I came to give her a hard time, she turned right around and told me I was welcome any time," Frank said. "Now that's a teacher we can be proud of."

Soon the tables had completely turned. Everyone was gathering around Violet and offering her their support.

"We still haven't settled the matter at hand," Thomas Brown bellowed. "Do we allow the child to attend classes or not?"

"Let's take a vote," Uncle Lath suggested.

"All those in favor of the Indian going to school say 'Aye,'" Thomas Brown said.

A handful of "ayes" sounded from here and there.

"All those opposed say 'Aye,'" Thomas said.

Again, only a few 'ayes' could be heard.

Thomas waited, unsure of how to proceed. It was a tie, with most people abstaining from voting.

Finally, Denis stood up. "If you are going to take anything out on someone, I'm the one to blame. I brought Miss Seymour here. I also rescued Gentle Lamb from the top of Maiden Rock." He paused. "I know it is no secret that I have never had any kind feelings towards the Indians. What you don't know is why."

Violet watched him. He was always so sure of himself, yet now he was so hesitant. She too had wondered about his reasons. Was he going to reveal them to everyone right here and now? And if so, what had changed his mind?

"I have hated the Indians for as long as I can remember," he said. "You all know that Uncle Lath and I came from Ohio. Well, so did the Keith family, including King and Caroline's niece, Violet Seymour."

He waited. Violet wished she could go grab his hand and offer him some moral support. Instead, she sat, awed by this man she couldn't understand, and waited with the rest of them for him to continue.

135

"I hated the Indians for what they did to me," he said. His voice caught in his throat, not finding a way of escape. Finally he said, "My mother and father were both killed by Indians. They left their scalps on their beds."

Everyone gasped. There had been a great deal of gossip about Denis MacLeod's hatred for the Indians, but no one had suspected such a thing as this.

"I was only three years old at the time," Denis said. "I hid under the bed and watched..." His voice trailed off. He could not speak any more.

"So you agree?" Kate Webster asked. "You don't think we should let them into the school either?"

"A month ago I would have set fire to their teepees rather than let them mingle with our own kind," Denis said. He looked at Violet and smiled. "But two women have taught me a great deal since then. Miss Seymour has taken Gentle Lamb under her wing and has nurtured her, treating her like she was her own flesh and blood."

He stopped again. Violet beamed at him. She was not tired now. Her mind was reeling, but it was with pride in this man she knew she was falling in love with. Never had she felt about anyone as she did about Denis MacLeod at this moment.

"And the other woman, a little one, is Gentle Lamb herself. When I found her, she was like a lost sheep. She blamed herself for the death of her sister and Rattling Leaf. I know that feeling of guilt myself. Even as a three-year-old, I thought I should have been able to stop them. Oh, I know that if they had found me they would have killed me too. I could not forgive them. It was not until I met Miss Seymour and Gentle Lamb that I was able to forgive myself."

Everyone sat in dead silence. It was hard to imagine what a mere child must have suffered all these years. No one would blame him if he continued hating the Indians. Certainly they had given him adequate reason for hating them.

"As I looked at Gentle Lamb and felt her cling to me like I was her only hope, I realized that it was not her fault that others had died, no more than it was my fault that my own parents died. She is only a child! For God's sake, can't you see? If we can teach these children—while they still are children—how to live in harmony with us, then maybe our life won't be so bad, even with their teepees lining our streets."

After a long silence, Thomas Brown got up. "Are there any objections to Gentle Lamb staying in school?" he asked.

"Nay!" everyone said in unison. Everyone except Kate Webster. She said nothing. Even a Webster knew when they were licked.

As the meeting was closed, Violet walked over to Denis. She smiled up at him warmly, her eyes dancing with the admiration she felt for him.

"May I be so bold as to ask for your company on the way home?" she asked.

Denis laughed. It was unheard of for a woman to approach a man in such a manner, but Violet Seymour was not just any woman. He knew that the day he rescued her from the waters of Lake Pepin.

"Welcome to Lake City," he said, taking her hand in his. He grinned broadly. "I think they like you."

"And they practically adore you," Violet said, winking at him, "and I can't imagine why!"

CHAPTER 20

"Why don't you take the carriage home?" Denis asked Arnold. "I think I will walk Mistress—Violet—home. I, um, think we both need some fresh air to clear our heads."

"Sure," Arnold said. "I understand." That famous twinkle in his eyes was as glaring as ever.

Denis went over to Violet and took ahold of her elbow. "Shall we go?" he asked.

"What about Mr. Bowen?" Violet asked. "Is he ready to leave?"

"He's going on his own," Denis answered. "I've already talked to him."

"And why is that?" Violet asked, afraid of the answer.

"I thought the fresh air would do us both good," he explained. "In case you hadn't noticed, it's been a pretty rough night—for both of us."

"It has, hasn't it?" Violet said. She looked at him with admiration. She had wondered so often about Denis's hatred for the Indians, but she had never imagined anything as cruel as what he had endured. Her heart broke at the thought of Denis, as a cute little three-year-old, cowering under the bed, watching the massacre of his own parents.

Her thoughts turned to Uncle Lathrop. She gathered that he had never married, yet he had taken on the responsibility of raising his nephew. He had done well, she had to admit. In spite of the scars he had carried for all these years, Denis truly was about the kindest man she had ever known. His actions with Gentle Lamb were proof of that. His two-facedness was so explainable, once she understood him.

"Ready?" Denis asked, waiting for her to come to the end of her daydream.

"Yes," she said simply, walking side-by-side with the man who had made her so proud tonight.

They walked in silence. Funny, she thought, how sometimes you don't have to say a word and yet there are volumes being said between you. She had never known such an experience with anyone before.

The air was crisp with the coolness of the rapidly approaching winter. The smell of autumn seemed to be everywhere.

Denis stopped at the edge of a grove of trees and sat down on the damp ground, his back propped against a trunk. He grabbed Violet by the hand and pulled her down beside him. She willingly obliged. She laid her head against his shoulder, feeling the warmth of his breath on the top of her head and the beat of his heart thundering within his chest.

"I was so proud of you tonight," she said, finally breaking the silence.

"Why?" Denis asked. "I made a complete idiot out of myself."

"Did not," Violet said. "It took a lot of courage to get up in front of all of your friends and say what you did." She took his hand in hers and said, "I'm so sorry. It must have been very painful."

"Let's talk about something else," he said.

"Like skunks?" she asked, smirking at him.

"You're mean!" he said, pushing her away from him but laughing all the time.

~*~

Gentle Lamb crawled out of the bush she had been hiding in and crept silently back to the Bowens' house. She had carefully snuck out after Mrs. Bowen thought she was asleep. She made her way to the schoolhouse and crouched down below the back window to hear what they were discussing. She had to strain her ears—and her mind—to get the gist of what they were all saying.

She didn't understand everything, but she could tell they were talking about her. She was the only Indian in school today, so there was no doubt in her mind that she was causing all the troubles Spring Flower was having.

Once she was out of their sight, she ran as fast as her pudgy little legs would carry her. The thoughts in her mind raced as fast as her feet. She had ruined everything for Spring Flower. And poor Arms-of-Steel! Her own people had killed his mother and father. How could he be so kind to her? She had heard that he hated her people. Who could blame him? Now Arms-of-Steel had pushed Spring Flower away from him. She shivered as she ran. She had watched her grandfather treat his mother like that so many times. My father, she thought, was so much more of a man than my grandfather. He was always kind and tender to her mother, and he had treated her, his oldest child, like a little princess. She had heard Mr. Bowen say that Arms-of-Steel loved Spring Flower, but she had to do something to protect her. She could not stand the thought of Spring Flower being mistreated. She had to do something.

She scurried into bed, leaving her clothes on except for her leather beaded moccasins. She buried her head in the pillow, trying to stifle her sobs. She had trusted Denis. She couldn't think of him as "Arms-of-Steel" anymore. He had saved her life, but for what? She had felt so secure with the two of them. Her whole life had crumbled right in front of her eyes tonight.

~*~

Denis and Violet sat under the tree for hours before they realized how late it had gotten. He had taken his jacket and wrapped it around her. It doesn't feel nearly as warm as his arms, Violet thought.

"We really should be getting home," Violet said. "I have to get up for school tomorrow."

Denis hesitated, then asked, "What about Gentle Lamb?"

"What about her?" Violet asked.

"Are you going to take her?"

"Of course," Violet said, pounding her fist on her lap. "I think, after your speech tonight, that she will be accepted just the same as any other child."

"I hope you're right," Denis said softly. "I hate to think of her being mistreated."

Violet tilted her head to look up into his deep eyes. He was the kindest man she had ever known, in spite of her first impressions of him. She had thought him arrogant, bigoted, stuck on himself—the list could go on and on. How wrong first impressions can be, she admitted.

"I suppose you're right," Denis said. "I promised Arnold I would help him with that house tomorrow."

"That is an awfully big house," Violet said. "How does he plan to move it?"

Denis laughed. "I wondered the same thing, but you know Arnold Bowen. If there is any way to do it, he'll figure it out."

"So did he?" Violet asked.

Denis laughed again. "He sure did."

Violet waited. When Denis didn't explain, she said, "Care to tell me how?"

"Sure," Denis said. "That's what he did today—got it ready for moving. He said it would take more than a dozen horses to haul it across town the way it was, so he sawed the blame thing in half. Right down the middle. He built a giant dray under each half of the house. He will hitch the horses to the dray and away we go."

"I want to see that," Violet said, excited by the thought of a half a house going right through the middle of town.

"I expect everybody will want to see it," Denis said. "When you see it coming, you better let the kids out for recess. You won't be able to control them inside anyway."

"You're probably right," Violet said. Suddenly she remembered her dream. She smiled at the thought of Denis dealing with their four imaginary children. Would it ever come to that? Did she dare hope?

Denis walked Violet home. He kissed her gently on the cheek and said simply, "Good night." Then he disappeared around the corner, headed directly for his and Uncle Lath's house. She watched, and even though she could not see him any longer, she could still hear him whistling, the way he always did when he was happy. Her heart skipped a beat. She had never been so happy. She didn't know she could feel this way.

Violet carefully put the brace across the back door and went quietly upstairs. She didn't want to awaken anyone. She pulled the white muslin curtains open just enough to let a little moonlight in. She didn't want to disturb Gentle Lamb. It was late.

Gentle Lamb lay still, afraid to breathe because she was sure she would start to cry again. She didn't want anyone to know that she had been spying on them.

Violet lay in bed, staring up at the moonlight reflecting off the ceiling. She tried to stop them, but the tears ran freely down her cheeks, leaving their stains on her fresh white pillow slip.

It had been years since Violet had allowed the liberty and cleansing crying offered her. She could not even remember her own parents. Now she knew that Denis had grown up not knowing his either, yet the vision of their murders were so horrendous that he could never forget it. Her heart ached for him.

Gentle Lamb could not sleep. When she heard Violet, she turned over to face her. She wrapped her arms around her neck, saying softly, "Nobody will hurt you. Gentle Lamb will watch over you."

Violet smiled through her tears. "Nobody is going to hurt me," she assured her.

"I know," Gentle Lamb said. Yes, she knew. She had heard them at the schoolhouse. She had seen Denis push her away from him, and it was all her fault. She didn't know what to do about it, but she had to do something.

Tomorrow, she told herself in the darkness as she finally drifted off to sleep. Tomorrow I will figure out what to do.

Violet slept, but her dreams were not of sugarplums, nor of curly red-headed children. No, her dreams were nightmares of Indian savages chasing after little children. She had to protect them. She would formulate a plan—tomorrow. She was here to educate the children of Lake City, and she would do it, come hell or high water. It was payback time for what they had done to Denis.

He deserved far better. She had to make it up to him for his parents' death. She owed him that much. She owed him her life. Tomorrow...

~*~

The morning dawned and Violet was up and dressed long before Mrs. Bowen even started breakfast. The house was silent. Too quiet. She sat on the little cane rocker in the corner by the window and stared out into space. Her mind whirled. Would Mrs. Webster cause trouble? Had Black Cloud heard about the meeting last night? Would he try to take it out on Denis? Now he would know why Denis hated his people so much. Would he assume that there was some logical reason for his parents' death? Would he go after Denis to finish the job the others had started?

"I love you," Gentle Lamb said, crawling up onto Violet's lap. "Please don't be sad."

Violet ran her hand over her long thick black hair. How did such a tiny child get so wise?

"I'm not sad," Violet said.

"You look sad," Gentle Lamb said.

"I am—worried," Violet said. She felt comfortable sharing her innermost thoughts with this tiny new person who had come into her life. She could hardly remember what it had been like before her. "Empty" was the only word she could think of to describe it. She smiled at her new little charge. "I love you too," she said reassuringly. There was no way she could know that Gentle Lamb was privy to all the events of the night before.

"Don't worry," Gentle Lamb said. "We'll figure it out together." She giggled. "Led taught me that," she explained. "He says if we stick together we can figure out anything."

"You're right," Violet said. "We will figure it out together." You and me and Denis, she thought. Together we can handle anything.

Violet gently pushed the child up, saying "You'd better hurry up and get dressed for school. I hear Mrs. Bowen downstairs."

"I'm not going to school," Gentle Lamb said.

"And why not?" Violet asked.

"I—um—I think I'm going to be sick," Gentle Lamb said.

Violet chuckled. "And what makes you think you are going to be sick? Do you have an in with the gods who tell you ahead of time what is going to happen?"

"I...don't understand," Gentle Lamb said.

"Never mind," Violet said, "but as long as you don't feel bad yet, you are going to school." Gentle Lamb's bottom lip began to tremble. "If we are going to figure things out together, we have to be together."

"I guess so," she finally conceded. She grabbed her dress and pulled it on over her head. She quickly slipped into her moccasins and started towards the door. "I'm ready."

Violet grabbed her hand and swung it as they walked down the corridor and the stairway.

"Well, you certainly look chipper this morning," Arnold Bowen said. "Any special reason?"

"We've figured out that we're going to figure out things," Gentle Lamb said, grinning proudly at her use of the strange new language she was learning.

"Then it will be figured out," Arnold said.

Led skipped into the living room, acting exactly like any other six-year-old, in spite of his mother's glare.

"Can I help figure it out too?" he asked.

"Nope," Gentle Lamb said. "This is—girl stuff." Oh, yes, she thought. I saw how Denis treated Violet. You can't trust a man, maybe not even Led. She wanted to, so desperately, but she wasn't sure she should.

"Okay," Led said, going out to the kitchen. "I'm hungry."

"Just like a man," Violet said, laughing. "The most important thing in life is food."

Mrs. Bowen set the griddlecakes, bacon and the large bowl of scrambled eggs on the table. She poured the tea and waited while they dished the food onto their plates. When everyone was ready to eat, she no sooner sat down than there was a knock at the front door. She jumped up and hurried to see who was there so early.

"Good morning," Denis said cheerfully. "'Tis a fine day for...whatever."

Arnold caught the twinkle in Denis's eyes. "And whatever can be dangerous," he warned. "Violet, if I were you, I would watch him very carefully today."

"Every day," she said, smiling at him.

CHAPTER 21

Violet sighed with relief when she saw that no one was at the school yet. Maybe, she prayed, things would go as normal.

She laughed. One day of school, one night of chaos and she thought a pattern was already established. Reality told her that anything could happen—at any time.

"Looks okay," Gentle Lamb said, as if she could read her thoughts.

"You are too wise for your years," Violet said. "I don't know how I ever got lucky enough to find you."

Gentle Lamb giggled. "You didn't find me. Arms-of-Steel did."

A shiver went up and down Violet's spine. She could feel Denis's arms around her—when he had rescued her from Lake Pepin, when he had held her close beneath the oak tree. They were truly arms of steel; they made her feel safe. Surely Gentle Lamb felt the same warmth from those muscle-bound appendages.

"You really like him, don't you?" Violet asked, setting her books on the desk and starting to write the A-B-C's on the slate board.

Instead of the enthusiastic response she expected, Gentle Lamb remained silent.

"What's the matter?" Violet asked, sensing that something was bothering her special little friend.

"Nothing," Gentle Lamb said, turning away from Violet.

"Come here," Violet said, sitting in her desk chair. "You know you can tell me anything. Remember, we can figure out anything— as long as we are together."

"Not this," Gentle Lamb said softly.

"What has Denis done to upset you so much?"

"Nothing," Gentle Lamb answered again. She was glad when the Webster children appeared, knowing that Violet would not continue questioning her with others there.

Soon the other children began arriving. Led had stayed behind to help his father with the chores, but he was in plenty of time to ring the bell again.

"I want to ring it!" Willie Webster begged.

"Okay," Violet said, "but just today. We will trade off every day."

"Me tomorrow!" someone shouted. "It's my turn!" another child yelled.

Violet looked around. Just off-view of the window stood Frank Patton.

"Tomorrow is Frank's turn," Violet said. "That is, if he comes inside and does the lessons today."

Frank bowed his head, embarrassed at being spotted. He really did want to learn, but he figured he could do it from outside. Now he had been found out.

"Come on in," Violet invited. Slowly, shyly, Frank went around to the door and made his way through the door.

Violet looked around. There was only one problem. Uncle Lon had not counted on someone as big as Frank attending the new school. She knew it would be another catastrophe if he tried to squeeze into one of the desks.

"Will you sit up here?" Violet asked, placing a chair beside the front row. "I'm not very tall, you know, and if I need help, I could sure use you."

"Yes, Mistress Seymour," Frank said, smiling proudly.

Violet smiled at him. He really didn't deserve the reputation he had gotten. He wasn't a bad kid; he just needed somebody to give him a chance.

She gave the lessons for the first half of the morning, then announced recess. The children all raced to get outside. It was a beautiful day, with just a bit of autumn chill in the air. Soon, she thought, it will be too cold for them to play outside.

She busied herself with work inside for the fifteen minutes, then called the children to return. She had tried to keep an eye on Gentle Lamb. Yesterday she had played with the other children happily and gaily. Today she remained alone, not talking to the others, even when they invited her to join them in a game of tag.

Inside, during the classes, Violet saw that Gentle Lamb was writing everything when she was told to, but she would not answer any questions, even when Violet asked her directly. Something was wrong—terribly wrong—but how could she get her to confide in her?

Before she knew it, it was time for lunch. The children scrambled to get their lunches and eagerly dug into their sandwiches, cookies, and whatever other goodies their mothers had packed for them.

The clip clop, clip clop of a horse sounded off in the distance. Violet went to the window to see who was coming. The horse was barely in view when she knew it was Denis. Her heart skipped a beat, knowing she would soon be face-to-face with him.

"I brought you something," he said, jumping down from his horse and unloading a cotton bag. He called the children to him, then dumped the bag full of sweet, juicy red apples onto the ground. The children grabbed for them, several boys reaching for the biggest ones and ending up in a fight.

"Enough!" Denis shouted. "There are plenty here for everyone."

The boys slowly relinquished their hold on the one big red orb and took a smaller one in its place. Frank Patton, Denis saw, ended up with the premium. He smiled, content with the knowledge that his friend from yesterday's fiasco was the victor.

He suddenly realized that he had not seen Gentle Lamb there. He looked around the playground for her, finally spotting her sitting all alone behind a bush. He sauntered over to her, smiling as he got closer.

"Care for an apple?" he asked, rubbing it against his pants leg to shine it up.

She reached for it, shyly, then changed her mind.

"No thank you," she said, not daring to look at him.

"Want to tell me what's troubling you?" he asked, sitting down on the ground beside her.

"Nothing," she said, knowing he would not believe her.

"Not likely," Denis said. "I haven't seen you act like this since the day I rescued you up on Maiden Rock."

"It doesn't matter," she said, wishing he would leave and go question somebody else.

"It matters to me," Denis said. "I don't like failure. If the person I saved is unhappy, it means I have failed. Now, shall we try again?"

They were interrupted by the children all yelling and shouting and running out to the road and pointing at something which had just come into view. Denis got up and went to see what was causing such a commotion.

Violet, still inside the schoolhouse, heard the noise too and came running outside. She bumped into Denis on the way. He reached out to steady her, causing her heartbeat to increase tenfold.

"What's happening?" she asked.

Denis laughed. He had been helping Arnold Bowen with his house moving job until almost noon. Arnold told him to take a break, and he would see him later. It was, Denis had to admit, the funniest plan he had ever seen anyone attempt.

The old Rahilly house, which was huge by any standards, was to be moved from the edge of Sugar Loaf to Lake City proper. It had been bought by two different families. The Hampstens had gotten one half of it, and that was the half Arnold was moving first. Denis and several other men had been working all morning with him to get it secured to the drays so it was ready to be pulled.

Now it was on its way. Eight of the biggest, strongest horses in town had been loaned for the pulling. Even they struggled against such a heavy load.

As the house got closer to the school, the children began to laugh. As soon as Violet saw it, she could not keep from joining them. There, in the living room, was Maude Hampsten on her hands and knees. She had a scrub brush in one hand and was steadying herself with the other. Directly in front of her was a bucket of hot, sudsy water. Not to be negligent in readying her new house, she was scrubbing the floors as the house wound its way from the bluffs to town.

When it was past and nearly out of sight, Denis turned to Violet. He loved the way she laughed. It made her freckles stand out a little more than usual. Her nose twitched, like it possessed the magic of an Irish leprechaun.

"I have to get over there to help him," he said reluctantly. He wished he had the nerve of Frank Patton. Maybe he could fake his ability to read and write so he could come and sit under her instruction every day. He smiled at the thought.

"Go," she said. "I think I can get them back under control." She laughed again. "Have you ever seen anything funnier?"

"No," Denis admitted. "I would think this will go down in Lake City history as one of the most amusing days we have ever had."

Violet looked around. "Have you seen Gentle Lamb?" she asked Denis.

"She was over there behind the bushes," he said, pointing in the general direction where he had found her earlier.

"She's been acting really strange," Violet confided in him. "I'm worried about her."

"I know," Denis agreed. "I tried to find out what was bothering her."

"Did she tell you?" Violet asked.

"No," he said. "Nothing." He took his watch out of his pants pocket, the bright gold chain catching the sun's rays and glistening brightly. "I do have to get over to help Arnold, but I will try to talk to her tonight."

"Maybe if we talked to her together," Violet suggested.

"Good idea," Denis said, winking at her as he headed for his horse. Any excuse to spend more time with Violet was a good idea. "I'll see you this evening."

"It's a date," Violet said, then blushed deeply. She hadn't meant to say that. She certainly was not in the habit of asking a man for a date, especially not one that made her as nervous as Denis MacLeod.

CHAPTER 22

By the time school was out and Violet returned home the whole town was abuzz about Maude Hampsten scrubbing the floors as the house went through town. Mrs. Bowen was laughing with Led and Gentle Lamb about it when Violet came in. Violet was pleased to see Gentle Lamb in a better mood.

"You saw it too?" Mrs. Bowen asked.

"Everybody saw it," Violet said. "It was too funny for words."

"Now that's one for a Webster," Mrs. Bowen quipped. "Too funny for words!" For some reason the expression tickled her funny bone. "I wonder what Kate Webster had to say about it. They're cousins, you know. Kate and Maude, I mean."

Violet had often wondered if everybody in Lake City was related to everybody else. If not, she had finally decided, they would be by the time the next generation got done mating.

Violet watched Gentle Lamb carefully. Led seemed to be able to reach out to her when nobody else could. I'll have to talk to him later, she thought. She tucked the notion away for safekeeping, just like she had done with Denis's letter.

The letter. It surprised her that it had reared its head. She had nearly forgotten about it. It had been days since she had sat down carefully at the little secretary desk in her room after Gentle Lamb was fast asleep and wrote it down. She laughed at herself at the time. It was so useless. She knew it so well, even though it was no more. Lake Pepin had seen to that. She was afraid that some day, when she was old and feebleminded, she would have forgotten how beautiful the words had been.

Between Led and Denis and herself maybe they could get to the bottom of Gentle Lamb's problem. Maybe, she thought, it is just that the reality of all of the deaths had finally registered. Often, she knew, grief took time. If that was the case, she would have to try harder to be there for her new "daughter."

There was a scuffle out in the front yard. Mrs. Bowen hurried to the front door. There, right in the middle of her prize flower garden, were a whole gaggle of children, pulling and picking at the blossoms that had survived the fall weather.

"Get out of there!" she screamed, wildly waving her broom at them.

The children backed out of the flower beds, nearly tripping over one another, giggling in spite of Mrs. Bowen's apparent rage. Violet was always amazed at how such a tiny woman could sound so fierce.

Violet was surprised that the children did not run away, but went out to the edge of the yard and sat down on the ground.

Mrs. Bowen disappeared into the house, and in a few minutes she was back, armed with a plateful of sugar cookies and a brown ceramic pitcher of good cold milk.

Violet watched as she poured some of the milk into a glass and handed it to one after another, carefully rinsing it out between each child with the bucket of water Led had brought out. It was, Violet realized, a ritual—a tradition—for the children to congregate at the home of the Bowens every so often. Tuesday, she thought. Maybe it is every week on Tuesday.

When the children were finished with their treats, they politely thanked Mrs. Bowen and meandered off down the road.

"That was nice of you," she said as she helped Mrs. Bowen carry the things back inside.

"Humph!" she sputtered. "If I didn't do that, they would probably attack the house." Her eyes twinkled, just like her husband's, at such a thought. She loved the children, and they all knew it. Her home was a regular haven to many of them when they faced problems. Already Violet had seen different ones come in the back door, their chins hanging nearly to their knees, then disappear after only a few minutes with a smile as big as all outdoors.

Perhaps Gentle Lamb would sense the trust the other children had in her and would allow her to help with her problems too. Violet hated the thought that this child who had become so dependent on her would not depend on her now. She was sure she could help, if given half a chance.

It was nearly time for dinner when Arnold came home. Close behind him was Denis, looking twenty years older than he had in the morning, Violet mused. He is soft, she thought. He was not used to the hard physical labor he must have endured helping Arnold move the Rahilly house. It could hardly be classified as hard physical labor—steering the ferry across the lake several times a day. Still, he had a good reputation for what he did, him and Uncle Lath.

They were well spoken of by everyone. Besides, Denis was just about the only eligible bachelor in Lake City, and there were quite a few single young maidens who would give their right arm to entice him into their corner. She had watched them, time after time, bat their eyelashes and tilt their heads from side to side, flirting shamelessly with him.

"Good evening, Denis," Mrs. Bowen greeted him cheerfully. "Joining us for dinner?"

"I asked him," Arnold said. "I knew you would have plenty."

Denis laughed, his head thrown back like always. Violet smiled, then joined him in the laughter. There was something absolutely infectious about that laugh. She forgot, momentarily, how worried she was about Gentle Lamb.

"Something funny?" Mrs. Bowen asked, seemingly irritated by the sudden outburst.

Violet and Denis exchanged worried glances.

"You might as well tell her," Arnold said. "Sooner or later somebody will."

"It is—you are—Arnold says," Denis said, stuttering uncontrollably, "you are the only person he ever knew who could have leftovers from food you never served the first time."

"Why, Arnold Congdon Bowen!" Mrs. Bowen shouted at her husband. "How could you say such a thing?" She bit her lips, trying to remain in control, but it was too late. Soon she too was laughing almost hysterically. "You, of all people, should know that a Scotsman can always make something out of nothing!"

"Aye, an' do it with high class," Denis said, bringing forth his best Scottish accent. "An' 'tis a fact of which ye kin be r-r-r-r-ight pr-r-r-r-oud of that fact."

They all laughed together. Led joined them, then finally Gentle Lamb. Violet looked at the child, feeling sorry for the fact that she probably didn't have a clue what was really so funny. Strange, how when one person laughs it gets everybody else joining in, even if they never got the punch line.

Arnold chided Violet as she picked away at her food, hardly eating anything. She and Denis had agreed to try to figure out what was bothering Gentle Lamb after they ate. The thought of being alone with him caused a mixture of emotions she could not explain, and she certainly didn't know how to cope with them. Part of her longed to be where he could kiss her again. She knew she would melt in his embrace. The other part of her shivered with fear. Fear of the unknown. Fear of the unexpected, the unexplainable.

Mrs. Bowen got up to clear the table and began to pour the water from the reservoir in the cookstove into the big tin dishpan. She peeled some of the homemade soap off the bar and swished it around with her hand. Violet got up and got a hand embroidered dishtowel so she could help her.

"You two young ones go on," Mrs. Bowen said, grinning knowingly at them. "I suspect you have some things to discuss."

"School," Violet said quickly, her face turning crimson.

"Business," Denis added.

"Monkey business," Arnold teased, winking at Denis.

They went out onto the front porch and sat in the swing. Neither of them said anything for quite some time. Violet counted the squeaks each time it went back and forth. Finally Denis broke the silence.

"She seems really upset about something."

"I know," Violet said. "She acted terribly withdrawn all day today."

"She's been through a lot," Denis said, his voice warm with sympathy. "The deaths, running away, living with strangers, a new language..."

"I thought about that too," Violet said. "Maybe it just hit her all at once. Sometimes it takes a while, you know."

"The problems of parenthood," Denis said, laughing. "At least you didn't have to go through labor pains to get there."

Violet fiddled nervously with the chain on the swing. The four children she had seen in her dreams popped into her mind's vision. Could he read her thoughts? She shook her head. It was impossible. It was more than that; it was dangerous! Such thoughts could make a man run for the woods, afraid of being trapped by some finagling female.

"I think we should go find her," he said. "Maybe if we both talk to her she won't be so afraid."

"Let's get Led to come with us," Violet suggested. "She seems to trust him."

They got up and walked back into the house.

"Led! Gentle Lamb!" Denis called out. No one answered.

Arnold and Mrs. Bowen came out into the living room.

"What's wrong?" Arnold asked. "Why do you need the children?"

"We just want to talk to them," Denis said.

Not wanting to worry them, Violet quickly added, "About school."

"They went out to play," Mrs. Bowen said. "I'll go see if I can find them."

Mrs. Bowen went outside and called to them. There was no answer. She waited, then called again. Still no answer.

"Desperate times call for desperate measures," she said. Then she put two fingers into his mouth and let out with the loudest, shrillest whistle you ever heard.

Violet and Denis both jumped.

~*~

"We'd better go," Led said, pulling Gentle Lamb by the hand down from the tree house. "Mother means business when she calls like that."

Gentle Lamb stood directly in front of Mrs. Bowen. She was shaking, and it was not from the cold which seemed to be setting in for the night.

"Here I am," she said, whimpering. "What did you want?"

"Denis and Violet want to talk to you," she said. "Something about school."

"Why don't we take a walk?" Arnold asked his wife, handing her her coat. "The fresh air will help us sleep good tonight."

They disappeared, leaving Denis and Violet alone with the two children. Denis looked at Gentle Lamb just in time to see her put her finger to her lips, warning Led not to say anything.

CHAPTER 22

"I'm sorry," Gentle Lamb said, her head hung low, before Violet or Denis had a chance to say a word.

"For what?" Violet asked, rubbing Gentle Lamb's shoulders gently. "You haven't done anything." She paused, then asked, "Have you?"

She began sobbing. Led sat by her side, looking on helplessly.

"Can't make any sense out of a crying female," Denis said, winking at Led. "They're the worst kind."

Gentle Lamb cried even harder.

"Whatever it is, you can tell us," Violet said, trying to encourage her to share her burden with them. When she still said nothing, she turned to Led. "Do you know what's troubling her?"

Led shrugged his shoulders, but he would not utter a word either. Denis wondered if Violet had seen Gentle Lamb's warning to keep silence just a few moments earlier.

"We can't help you if you won't tell us," Violet said, her voice sounding far harsher than she wanted it to. She didn't want to scare her. Then she would never talk.

"I love you," Violet said softly, "like you were my own daughter. I would never do anything to hurt you."

"I—I know," Gentle Lamb said, her voice choking between the sobs.

"Then please trust me," she urged. "I want to help you."

"I—I can't."

Violet looked at Denis. Couldn't he think of something to say? Maybe if he spoke to her in her own language.

As if he heard her, he began to question her in her own tongue, hoping to pry her secrets from within. Instead of helping, it seemed to make matters even worse. Violet felt her whole little body tense up beneath her touch.

"Led," Violet pleaded again, "can't you help us? I am sure she has told you."

"I can't," Led said, looking nearly as frightened as Gentle Lamb. "I promised."

"Sometimes we have to break promises," Denis said, "especially if it will hurt the person we promised."

"I'd never hurt her!" Led shouted, jumping up.

An idea hit Violet. Had Gentle Lamb seen Black Cloud somewhere? Had he hurt her? Gentle Lamb was deathly afraid of him. If he had touched her, Violet vowed she would scalp him herself.

"Have you seen your grandfather?" she asked.

Gentle Lamb shuddered. She didn't say anything, but shook her head vehemently.

"Has he had someone hurt you?" Denis asked, seeing the direction Violet's thoughts were going.

Again silence, but she shook her head in denial.

"Has someone hurt you?" Violet asked.

Again no answer, but this time she did not shake her head.

Violet looked at Led. "Please tell us," she begged.

"I told you, I can't," he said, "at least not now."

"Then when?" Denis demanded. "How long do we have to wait to find out what is eating her insides out?"

"Maybe later," Led said, watching Gentle Lamb's reaction. "I— I don't know."

"This is getting us nowhere," Denis said disgustedly. "Led, take her in the house. I have to talk to Mistress Seymour alone."

Led took Gentle Lamb's hand and obediently took her inside. As soon as they were gone, Violet said, "Well?"

"Well what?" Denis asked. "Darned if I know. She's scared to death of something, but I don't know how to find out what it is. Unless..." He stopped in mid- thought.

"Unless what?" Violet asked. "I'm willing to try anything. I can't stand to see her in such pain."

"Maybe if I talk to Led alone. You know, man to man."

"It's worth a try," Violet said, willing to do anything. "I'll go in with her and send him out to see you."

They tried their separate inquisitions, but neither one made any headway. The only thing Violet gained from Gentle Lamb was her admission "It's nothing you did. I love you too, but..." And then she stopped.

"But what?" Violet asked, praying that she would continue her sentence.

"Nothing," Gentle Lamb said. "Just be careful."

Violet finally gave up in despair and went back out to Denis. It was obvious that he wasn't having any luck either. Led ran into the house as soon as she returned.

Denis went back over to the swing and sat down, motioning for Violet to join him. They pondered and discussed what to do about the little girl they had both grown so fond of. Before long their words escalated into an argument.

"She's still an Indian!" Denis said, his voice sounding harsh.

Violet was so sure his attitude had changed towards these people. She thought Gentle Lamb had accomplished that, but it was evident now that he was the same as ever. She remembered her Grandfather Benjamin Keith saying, "You can't change the spots on a leopard." Well, apparently you couldn't change Denis MacLeod's lofty ideas, either.

"She's just a little girl," Violet insisted.

"But she's an Indian!" he argued. "She's a Redskin. None of them are any different. Not even Gentle Lamb. You can't trust any of them."

"Don't say that!" Violet said, raising her voice to emphasize her aggravation with him. "You don't know anything at all about what you are saying."

"Oh, don't I? Who was it that killed my mother and father? Who taught me to hate them? They brought it all on themselves! I should never have brought her back here. She'd have been better off up there on the top of Maiden Rock until she died."

"Don't say that!" Violet screamed, then stomped away to the door. Denis followed her, but she was quick to set the lock in place. She ran to the back door, bolting it as well.

159

"Let me in!" Denis called out, banging on the door.

"Go away," Violet called back.

Finally, when he saw it was useless, he walked away, his head hung down dejectedly, back to his own home. Why did he have to let this burning hatred for the Indians ruin everything? Violet was the best thing that had ever happened to him, and now he had destroyed that too. Those blamed Redskins had a way of destroying everything, even when they weren't around. He found himself hating Gentle Lamb, and that scared him. Violet was right. She was just a child. It wasn't fair to put the blame on her for something that had been building inside him for years.

~*~

"Looks like you got hit by a low blow," Uncle Lath said as Denis stepped inside their house.

Denis ignored the comment. He didn't feel like talking. He didn't feel like anything. Damned funny, he thought, that one little woman can take every ounce of caring right out of you. Maybe it wasn't the Indians who were to blame for messing up the whole world. Maybe it was women.

"Lover's spat?" Uncle Lath asked.

"Naw," Denis muttered. "I ain't had this much fun since the pigs et my little brother."

Uncle Lath laughed at the use of the phrase he hadn't heard for years. It had been one of Denis's father's favorites.

Denis stomped on past him and kicked his boots off. He lay down on his bed, his clothes still on, and began pounding on his chest.

"Damn broad!" he sputtered, then rolled over, hoping sleep would overtake him and he could forget all about it—all about her.

~*~

Violet had told the Bowens about the problem she was having. Mrs. Bowen tried to talk to Gentle Lamb, but she got no farther than Violet and Denis had. Finally, Violet ordered Gentle Lamb

160

up to bed, and she busied herself with the lessons for the next day.

Concentration was almost impossible. She felt like such a failure. She couldn't communicate with her new "adopted" daughter. She had communicated too much with Denis, sending him off in a rage. How could she hope to influence the lives of all the children in Lake City when she couldn't even control her own life?

She finally slipped into the bed beside Gentle Lamb. She reached over for her, placing her hand on the child's arm. In her fitful sleep, Gentle Lamb curled up beside her, reaching out in her subconsiousness for the love and protection only Violet could give her.

"I love you," Violet said, knowing that Gentle Lamb could not hear her. "I love you too, Denis," she said, wishing he could hear her from across town.

CHAPTER 22

Violet hardly slept, spending most of the night hours trying to figure out a way to pry Gentle Lamb's secret from within. She would have to get it from Led. That was the only way. Or maybe, if she was lucky, it would just pass. At last, after a dreadfully long time, the light began to pour into the window and she hurried to get up, pour the water into the basin, wash and get dressed for another day.

She had enjoyed the first two days of school. For the most part the children had been very well behaved. Even Frank Patton, she thought, smiling at the way she had persuaded him to "help" her. Why should today be any different? It can't be, she decided. Not if I am going to be fair to the other children. And to Denis. After all, it was his school.

Violet put her hand inside her camisole, reaching for the letter she had grown so fond of. She took it out, unfolded it and read it. The words were the same, but the effect fell far short of its usual impact. Her handwriting was meticulously perfect, but the flourishes of Denis's penmanship lent a certain flair that spelled excitement. The magic he had described was noticeably missing.

As Gentle Lamb began to stir, she refolded the letter and put it back next to her heart. She had the words locked deep inside, along with the memories of his arms around her. She snickered. Arms-of-Steel definitely suited him fine.

Before she went downstairs for breakfast, Violet heard Denis's voice. His presence at the Bowen home was getting to be a habit, one she could easily adjust to.

"I am going to go talk to Black Cloud," Violet heard him tell Arnold. "Maybe he knows what is going on."

Violet rushed to join them. She was glad that Gentle Lamb was still upstairs. She didn't want her in the middle of another discussion like this.

"You can't do that," Violet said, butting into the men's conversation.

"And just why not?" Denis asked, seemingly upset by the intrusion. She is an outsider, he thought, remembering how she had nearly caused an uprising when she had run her fingers over the paintings on the teepees.

"Just the mere mention of her grandfather's name last night sent her into a panic," Violet explained. "She is afraid of him. I know he has mistreated her."

"He is still her grandfather," Denis argued.

"Maybe she is right," Arnold said, taking sides with Violet. "There must be another way to handle it."

"There is," Violet said. "Led."

"Led?" Arnold and Denis asked in unison.

"She trusts him," Violet said. "Perhaps he is the only one she trusts any more."

"What about you?" Denis asked.

"You saw how she clammed up last night with me. With us."

"I will question him," Arnold said. "He has always been a good boy. He will tell me—if he knows, of course."

They dropped the subject as soon as they spotted Gentle Lamb. They had not seen her a few moments earlier, listening to them discuss her.

"Good morning, Gentle Lamb," Denis said warmly, reaching down to lift her into his arms like he had done countless times.

Instead of the anxious response she usually had, she pulled away and clung to Violet's skirt.

"Are you ready for breakfast?" Violet asked, trying not to focus on her behavior.

Gentle Lamb nodded. They all went into the kitchen to sit down for the first meal of the day.

"I have to get to school early," Violet said as they finished eating. "Are you coming with me?"

Gentle Lamb looked pleadingly at Led.

"I'll bring her with me," Led said, reaching out and taking her hand.

"Then I'll accompany you," Denis said. "I am headed that way anyway. I really have to get back to work on the ferry. Poor Uncle Lath. I've left him alone for several days. Not that he can't handle it, but it is my job."

Gentle Lamb's eyes were filled with fear again. "Maybe I better go with you," she said to Violet.

"No," Violet said. "You go with Led. That's fine."

She noticed her uneasiness, but she still couldn't get to the bottom of the cause. She wasn't so sure that the four pudgy little imps in her dream were such a good idea after all. She couldn't even handle the one child she had "inherited." What right did she have to bring some other poor unsuspecting baby into the world when she wouldn't be able to manage them either?

As they walked, she was aware of Denis talking, but the words drifted over her head, ignored by the thoughts that echoed within her own mind. He finally walked out in front of her, stopped dead in his tracks and leaned forward, planting a huge, passionate kiss on her lips.

Violet jumped in surprise. It was broad daylight. People might be watching them. He had no right to do this to her. She had no right to enjoy it so much. They had no right to share such intimacy—openly. She had no right to be thinking the things she was thinking—secretly.

When he finally released her she gasped, coming up for air. He managed to knock the wind right out of her when he did things like this. Actually, he had the same effect on her when she was just near him. Her heart was churning within her like it would burst through her skin.

"You—you—you shouldn't do that!" she said.

He threw his head back like he always did when he laughed. His voice boomed from deep within his chest.

"Can you honestly tell me you didn't like it?" he teased.

"I—we—people might see us. They will talk. It isn't proper. I'm the school teacher. People—respect me. They should respect me. They should have...unless they saw..."

"So I embarrassed you?" he asked, his eyes aglow with the fire of passion he felt in his innermost being.

"You have to quit, you know," Denis said.

"Quit what?" she asked innocently.

"Quit trying to solve the problems of everybody in the whole world." He hesitated. "You can't, you know. Nobody expects you to."

"Gentle Lamb does," she argued. "She trusts me. At least she used to. Something has changed."

"She will again. Just give her time."

"How can you be so sure? About Gentle Lamb. About everything." About us, she wanted to add, but stopped before she said it.

"You'll see. It might take some time, but it will happen. She will come to you again."

Violet thought about the way she had crawled up next to her last night. The way she had turned to her for safety—even if it was in her sleep. It had to show that she did trust her, if she would just let herself.

They arrived at the schoolhouse. Denis pushed the door open. Violet smiled. There at the front of the left hand row of desks was a full-sized school desk. Frank Patton's desk. Uncle Lon had obviously been here already this morning.

Violet's thoughts turned to her Uncle King and Aunt Caroline. She had spent very little time with them lately. She had been so busy. She would go over to visit them after school. Maybe Aunt Caroline could give her some advice. She could sure use some. Yes, that was a good idea. There had to be a solution to all her problems. Maybe it lay with her own family, her own flesh and blood.

~*~

Rose Petal watched from behind the lilac bush, where she knew she was safely hidden from view. When she was satisfied that everyone was gone but Mrs. Bowen, she quietly walked up to the back door and walked inside the back entry so she would not be seen when she knocked softly on the inner door. Mrs. Bowen came quickly, ushering her inside before anyone spotted them.

Rose Petal sat at the kitchen table and waited for Mrs. Bowen to bring the tea and cookies for what was becoming their morning ritual. No one had any idea that the two women communicated daily as best they could, considering their language differences. "Once a mother, always a mother," Mrs. Bowen told Rose Petal.

Rose Petal was quick to learn many English words, and Mrs. Bowen found herself picking up quite a few Sioux words. She loved the sound of the foreign words as they rolled off her tongue. Rose Petal smiled, delighted both by her new friendship and her attempts at learning her native language.

The two women shared a common interest: they both loved Gentle Lamb without reservation.

Rose Petal's eyes clouded over as she learned that something was troubling her daughter, but she did not know how to approach Gentle Lamb without putting her at risk, as Black Cloud would surely retaliate if he saw the two of them together.

Suddenly, an idea struck Rose Petal. "Gentle Lamb has her giveaway?" she asked Mrs. Bowen.

"What is her giveaway?"

"The medicine wheel she wears around her neck," Rose Petal explained. "It belonged to Little Flower before..."

Mrs. Bowen watched, feeling utterly helpless as Rose Petal wept, not from the loss of one of her daughters, but from losing both of her daughters. When she was composed enough to speak again she continued, choosing her limited vocabulary carefully.

"When Little Flower went to the Great Beyond I took her necklace off her. It was made by her grandmother." Rose Petal stopped momentarily. Mrs. Bowen was sure she was trying to find the right words. Her heart reached out to her, offering unspoken courage to continue.

"It is a wikpeyapi—a giveaway. When someone from our tribe goes on, they leave something behind for someone they loved, someone very special."

The tears rolled down Rose Petal's leathery cheeks as she spoke.

"Little Flower left too soon. She was too young. She could not speak her wishes, but she wanted Gentle Lamb to have her medicine wheel. She did not tell me, but I knew. A mother knows..."

Mrs. Bowen pushed her teacup aside and stood up, walking around the table to Rose Petal's side. She gave her a warm embrace. Rose Petal looked up at the tiny woman and smiled. "Thank you," she said simply.

"When someone receives a giveaway it is more than just an object. We believe that the spirit of the departed is left behind in the giveaway. The spirit of Little Flower lives on in Gentle Lamb. As long as she has the giveaway she is safe. Not even Black Cloud can harm her."

A big smile spread across Rose Petal's face. "Little Flower would have loved Wenona's new name. If only she could have known..."

Mrs. Bowen smiled back at her and grasped her work-toughened hand in both of hers. "She knows," she replied. "Just as you said a mother knows, so Little Flower knows."

~*~

The school day began as usual. Violet asked Gentle Lamb to ring the bell. She seemed pleased—for about five minutes, then she was withdrawn again for the rest of the day.

"Will you take Gentle Lamb home?" she asked Led after school. "I am going over to see Aunt Caroline. I won't be too long."

"Sure," Led said, taking his little Indian friend by the hand. "I like taking care of her."

Violet watched her carefully. She almost smiled. Maybe Denis was right. Maybe with time...

CHAPTER 23

Violet sat with Aunt Caroline at the kitchen table in their new home down in Little Scotland. She looked around. It was nice. Cozy. It was home. She felt a tinge of jealousy at not being part of the family any more. She felt like company, and she wasn't used to that at all. She would have to make it a point to come more often, no matter how busy she was.

"...Says it is just great," Aunt Caroline said.

"What?" she asked, oblivious to everything Aunt Caroline had said.

"I didn't think you were here," Aunt Caroline said, laughing. "So tell me, am I right?"

"About what?" Violet asked.

"I thought so," Aunt Caroline said. "Does he know?"

"Does who know?"

"Denis, of course."

"You aren't making any sense," Violet said, her cheeks a brilliant red. "Would you please explain?"

"Anybody who watches you can see that you are head over heels in love with him.

"With who?" Violet asked again, her voice considerably louder than was necessary.

"With Denis!" Aunt Caroline shouted back at her. "You can't be that blind!"

"I'm not blind," Violet insisted. "I'm not in love with..."

They were interrupted by a loud banging on the door. Before they could even go open it, Denis barged in, panting from the fast run he had just completed.

"You have to come, quick!" he said, dragging Violet by the hand and running out the door.

Aunt Caroline grabbed her coat and ran after them, but she was far too slow. They were nearly out of sight already.

"I wonder what that was all about," she said to herself, stroking the coat that was hung over her arm.

~*~

"What are you doing to me?" Violet asked, breathing harder than she had ever done before.

"It's Gentle Lamb," Denis said. "She's gone."

"Gone?" Violet asked. "Where?"

"I don't know," Denis said. "I just know Mrs. Bowen sent Arnold after me when she didn't come home from school with Led."

"But Led said he would take her home," Violet said. "He's such a good boy."

"But that's the point," Denis said. "He is a boy. He stopped to play aggies with some of the other lads. Gentle Lamb was with him when he stopped, but when he got up again she was gone. He figured she got tired of waiting and went on home."

Denis gasped for air, then continued.

"He went straight home, but she wasn't there."

"Where do you suppose she went?" Violet asked, overtaken with panic.

"Maybe she went to the teepees," Denis suggested. He headed for the Indian hovels which stood in the center of Lake City.

Violet listened as he rattled off questions in the native Sioux language. She couldn't understand a word of it, but she could read the expressions on their faces and see their heads shake "No." They would move on to the next teepee, where they would get the same response.

"Well?" Violet asked, exasperated by the fact that he didn't bother to tell her anything the people said.

"She was here earlier," Denis said, "but she left over an hour ago. Broken Branch said he saw her heading for the bluffs."

"No!" Violet shouted. "She could get lost up there."

"It's not likely," Denis said. "She knows that place like the back of her own hand."

Violet felt pangs of guilt. How was it that this child was in her charge, yet Denis knew more about her than she did? Of course she would know the bluffs. Everybody in Lake City knew the bluffs—everybody who had been there for a while, at least. But I don't know them, Violet thought.

"Come on," Denis said, again pulling her along behind him by her hand. "We'll get my horse and head up there. With a little bit of luck we will be able to go faster than she could."

"But she has a head start," Violet said, overtaken by fear. It was not the bluffs that frightened her; it was Gentle Lamb herself. She had been so withdrawn and despondent since yesterday. What if she did something foolish? Something like... No, she couldn't bring herself to even think such a thing. Maiden Rock was behind her. Gentle Lamb had to know how much she had come to mean to Violet. They had to reach her in time.

Denis ran out to the barn and grabbed the horse's reins. "Get on," he ordered Violet. He had never stopped to ask her if she knew how to ride. It didn't matter now. If she was behind him he could make sure she was safe.

She felt his big, strong hands encircle her waist, ready to lift her onto the horse's back. Her blood seemed to boil. Just moments ago she had been struck in the face by the cold, blustery wind. Now she was too hot to touch. Once she was settled in place, he mounted his faithful horse in front of her.

"Hang on!" he shouted, his heels biting into the side of the steed to spur him on as fast as possible.

Violet grabbed hold of his waist, hanging on for dear life. She had ridden a few times, but it had always been on a gentle old mare. This creature was as wild and untamed as Denis seemed right now. His hair blew in the wind, slapping her in the face from time to time. She would have brushed it away if she had dared to let go for even a second, but she knew if she relinquished her grip she would probably go flying.

They had barely gotten to the bottom of the bluffs when the snow began falling—slowly at first, then fast and furiously.

Violet wanted to yell at the heavens. Didn't God, or whoever was up there, know they had to find Gentle Lamb? They couldn't get waylaid now. This was far too important for some stupid snowstorm.

Before long Denis knew it was hopeless to try to go any further. He could not see more than a foot ahead of them. The horse was getting stubborn; he knew the danger all too well.

"We have to stop," he said.

"We can't," Violet argued. "We have to find her. If we don't, she could die."

"If we keep on, we could die too," Denis said. He had seen late fall blizzards before. They were as nasty as a tornado in Ohio.

"But we can't just stay here," Violet said, suddenly aware of just how cold it had gotten. The wind was blowing the snow in her face. She had not even taken time to get her coat from Aunt Caroline's. In the back of her mind, she remembered her aunt holding the coat out for her, calling to her, as she and Denis had left. Now she wished she had taken the few seconds it would have required to grab it.

"There are a lot of caves up here in the bluffs," Denis said. "We will have to go on foot, but with any luck we can find one."

He alit from the horse, then lifted Violet down to the ground. Her legs felt weak, like they were going to collapse beneath her.

"Are you all right?" he asked, not stopping to wait for an answer.

"Yes," she said, her voice barely audible. She struggled to keep up with him.

"I think there is one just ahead," Denis said, pulling the horse with one hand and Violet with the other. "Come on, Blackie," he urged the horse. Together, the three of them plowed through the thick, wet snow.

Denis felt along the wall of the bluff with his elbow.

"Here it is!" he cried out excitedly. "We can wait it out inside."

Violet did not argue. She trusted him—with her life. She could only pray that Gentle Lamb would find a cave where she could keep warm and dry overnight too. She had heard tales of how self-sufficient the Indians were. She had to believe that now, even if she had never done so before.

Denis went in first, followed by the horse and then Violet. He nearly tripped over a stick lying on the ground. He bent over to pick it up, pounded it into the ground and tied Blackie to it. He led Violet back farther into the cave. It was dark– so dark. Violet shuddered at the blackness of it.

When he felt that there was a wider spot, he struck a flint and held it up so they could see. As she looked around, Violet sensed that someone else had been there before. In one corner she spotted a heavy deerskin wrap. She went over to it, picked it up in spite of its weight, and tried to shake it out. The dust flew in every direction, making her cough. Denis came over and slapped her on the back. She coughed even harder. It hurt, but she would never tell him. He could do almost anything he wanted to. He had brought her to a place of safety. She was like putty in his hands. She was his for the taking.

She smiled in the semi-darkness. What made her think he would want to do anything to her? Oh, her imagination was far too vivid!

CHAPTER 24

"Wait in here," Denis said, heading back towards the opening in the cave. "I'm going to try to find some kindling twigs outside. We'll freeze to death if we don't get a fire going."

"I'm going with you," Violet said, following him.

"No," he insisted. "You will just slow me down, and I can't risk anything happening to you. I'm used to this; you're not."

Violet felt like one of her students after she had scolded them. She obediently sat down on the ground and pulled the wrap around her.

"Promise you'll hurry?" she asked.

"I promise," Denis said, smiling at her as he turned again and exited the cave.

A myriad of thoughts plummeted through Violet's mind as she sat there, alone, in the darkness. What if he falls out in the snow? How would I know where to look for him? It was snowing so hard his tracks would be covered in mere minutes. What about Gentle Lamb? Where is she? Is she safe? Why did she run away? Should we brave the elements of the first winter storm and continue our search for her?

It seemed like hours had passed when Denis finally returned.

"What took so long?" she asked.

He dropped the wood onto the floor and relit the flint. He pulled out his pocket watch, which glistened in what little light they had.

"A whole seven minutes," he said, laughing.

Violet grinned at him. How could he laugh at a time like this? But, she had to admit, she was glad he had. Anything seemed possible when he laughed that deep roar of a laugh, his head thrown back and his black hair glistening behind him.

"It seemed longer," she said simply.

"It doesn't matter," he said, arranging the sticks in a neat teepee shape ready for lighting. He took the flint and lit it carefully.

"We should have enough air in here, provided the snow doesn't block the entry."

Violet stirred at this suggestion.

"It won't snow that much," she said. "Will it?" The door was higher than she was. Denis had only had to stoop down a tiny bit to go through it. She had seen blizzards and storms in Illinois, but this one seemed much worse. More threatening, like it was striving to control everything around it.

"Can't tell," Denis said. "We can always hope."

"Yes," Violet said, "we can hope. I just hope Gentle Lamb has enough hope to survive too." Her eyes filled with tears over her concern for the tiny girl. "She seemed so sad," Violet said. "What have we done to her?"

"I don't think we have done anything," Denis said, "but you're right. Something sure is eating away at her."

"I wish she was here with us," Violet said. She shivered beneath the weight of the deerskin. It was so cold. Hopefully the fire would soon offer some warmth and relief.

Denis, responding to her needs, came over and sat beside her. He pulled the cover up over both of them, then put his arm around her, drawing her close against him.

"Feel better?" he asked. Oh, yes! She definitely felt better. At least to him.

"Yes," she said, "but I'm afraid."

"Of me?" he teased. "I won't bite."

"You might," she said, returning his banter. She sensed that he was trying to take her mind off the dangers that lurked outside for Gentle Lamb.

"Only if I get really hungry," he said, rubbing his hand on her arm to keep her warm. "You should have worn a coat."

"I know," she said, "but when you came to Aunt Caroline's all I could think about was going to find..."

Her voice drifted off like the snow blowing in the wind outside. Her eyes filled with tears. She shivered—from the cold and from what could be.

"She'll be all right," Denis promised, crossing his fingers symbolically of his own hope. "She has been raised to survive. She will."

"Oh, I hope you are right," Violet said. "I want to believe you. I really do."

"Have I ever been wrong before?" he asked.

Violet playfully slapped him lightly on the cheek.

"You are the most arrogant, pig headed, stubborn, maddening, exasperating man that ever lived," she snarled at him.

He bent over her and kissed her, his lips completely encompassing her mouth until she gasped for air.

"And you love every inch of me," he said, boasting of his own prowess like the king of the jungles.

"I do not!" Violet shouted. "I hate you! I hate the way you think you can solve anything. The way you think everything is in your control. Well, not this time. It's not. Gentle Lamb's very future and survival depends on her own wisdom and knowledge. You can't do a thing about it, no matter how hard you try or how much you want to."

"I'm sorry," Denis said sincerely. "I really am worried about her too. Not that she won't survive; I know she will, but I'm afraid for her to be alone. I don't know what has come over her, but I can't help but feel it is my fault."

"How can you say that?" Violet asked. "You have been the closest thing to a father she has known since..." She stopped, a catch in her voice. "That poor child! No one should have to endure such heartache and hardship."

Quickly changing the subject, Denis asked abruptly, "What ever happened to your mother and father? I have heard Uncle Lath talk of them, but he has never told me anything about where they went."

Violet's face waned. She had never spoken to anyone about them—other than Aunt Caroline and Uncle King, and of course Grandpa Benjamin and Grandmama Sarrah. It was so long ago, and she was so small. She closed her eyes tightly, trying to bring the mental image of them back. She filled with rage when she realized that they were gone—forever. She could not even remember what they looked like.

"You don't have to talk about it if you don't want to," Denis assured her.

"It's all right," she said slowly. "I think it might help."

He waited, holding her tightly to let her know he was there for her, yet not forcing her to do anything she wasn't ready for.

Slowly, quietly, she told him how her own parents had died on the way to Illinois. The trip had been hard, going on foot. She was just tiny, and her mother was not strong. When they passed a village plagued with typhoid, they could not withstand it. They both died in less than two days from the time they took ill.

"I'm so sorry," Denis said, stroking her bright red hair. "I wish I could help."

"You do," Violet said. "You are."

"I wish I had never brought you here," he said. "It is not fair for you to be holed up here in a cave with some strange man. I never meant for it to be like this."

"I know you didn't," Violet said. "You didn't force me to come to Lake City. It was my decision." She unbuttoned the top two buttons on her blouse and reached inside her camisole, pulling out the letter which meant so much to her. She tried to read it, but the light was not bright enough to make out the words. Still, from her heart, she began reciting the flowing phrases he had used to describe the place he loved so much.

"Where did you get that?" Denis asked.

"From you, silly," she said, laughing.

Denis laughed with her. He loved the look on her face when she laughed. Her little button nose turned up just a smidgeon and the freckles seemed to scrunch so close together that her face was as brown as if it was suntanned.

"I know that," he said, "but I sent it to King."

"He had lots of letters," Violet said. "I thought this one should be mine. After all, it was my invitation to Paradise."

"Some Paradise this turned out to be," Denis said, reaching toward the fire with a stick to be sure it didn't go out. "Bet you wish you had never heard of Lake City, or me, I'm sure."

176

"Just think of all the things I would have missed," Violet said, chuckling. "The water in Lake Pepin, walking down Main Street looking like a drowned rat, having an Indian come after me because I don't know enough to keep my fingers off his teepee, horrible smelling intruders at the school." She paused, watching the expression on his face. "Shall I continue?"

"I don't think so," Denis said. "I think I have heard quite enough."

"I would never have forgiven myself if I had not come here," Violet said. "I would never have had Gentle Lamb. I feel as if she is my own daughter." She gazed up at him, her big green eyes so wide they looked like they were ready to pop out of their sockets. "I would never have had...known...you."

"Count your blessings," he said sarcastically.

"I am," she replied. She tilted her head up slightly, put her arms around his neck and ran her fingers across her cheeks. "You're my biggest one."

Denis responded to her by kissing her again.

"Something wrong?" Denis asked, far too aware of the response she had triggered. "I told you I won't bite."

"But maybe you are hungry," she said, her face red even in the dim light from the fire.

"Oh, indeed I am," he said, kissing her neck, then her arms, then slowly, deliberately lifting the deerskin he had brought along for warmth and crawling in beside her, wrapping his arms around her to try to keep her warm.

As she drifted off to sleep, she lay with her wrapped in his arms, arms of steel, she mused, until they were both at peace—with one another and with the world.

"It's bound to be cold," he said, glancing at the fire.

Violet laughed. Her body was so full of his heat, of her own heat, she didn't think she would ever be cold again. She felt so safe in his arms.

One thing sure, she told herself, Denis MacLeod is a man of his word. He promised to show me Paradise. He has certainly done that! He was right; it was in Lake City. It was in the bluffs. It was deep inside a cave in the middle of a blizzard. It was, as he had written, "the closest place to heaven to be found here on earth."

Violet giggled. "We must be on Sugar Loaf," she said as she pulled the deerskin around her.

"What makes you think that?" he asked.

"Because it is certainly sweet," she joked.

"Indeed it is," Denis said. "Oh, yes, it is."

Sleep came quickly and easily for Violet. Her last words were, "Please, God, keep Gentle Lamb safe. And help us find her in the morning."

Denis echoed a heartfelt "Amen!"

He watched her as she slept, her face glowing from the light of the fire. There were no words to explain the yearnings he felt within himself. He knew he had to wait—wait until the time was right, but he also knew that he had to have this woman for the rest of his life. But first, they had to find Gentle Lamb.

CHAPTER 25

Uncle Lon, Uncle Lath and Uncle King began to worry when there was no sign of Denis or Violet and the wind was whipping angrily through the trees, blowing the snow so hard it made visibility a figment of their imagination. They made their way to the Bowens' house, hoping they might have gone there.

"We don't know where they have gone," Arnold Bowen told the "uncle threesome."

"Caroline said Denis came charging after Violet like a whirlwind, saying something about Gentle Lamb missing," Uncle King said.

"The wife said the same thing," Arnold confirmed. "Led was supposed to bring her home from school, but he stopped to play with some of the boys. She skipped out on him."

"Damned Redskins!" Uncle Lon grumbled. "They'll do that, no matter what. I've tried hiring some of them to help me with some jobs, but you can't depend on them."

"It's not her fault," Led said, cowering in the corner where they had not noticed him. "I should have known she'd do something like this."

"What do you mean?" Arnold demanded. "What do you know that you aren't telling us?"

"She…" He hesitated, knowing he was due for a good punishment for not telling them sooner. It was all his fault.

"Come on, out with it!" Arnold ordered.

"She said the whole big ugly fight in town was her fault. She…snuck out last night and went to the schoolhouse to listen. She heard everybody fighting about her being at school. She tried to get

Mistress Seymour to let her stay home, but she said she had to go to school. She felt awful. Then she saw Denis push her."

"Saw Denis push who?" Uncle Lath asked.

"Mistress Seymour. She said they were fighting too, and it was about her. She said if she was dead everybody could be happy."

"My God!" Arnold exclaimed. "The poor child! I don't know what that was all about, but I know Denis MacLeod well enough to know that he is so much in love with our schoolmarm that he can't even see straight. He would never do anything to hurt her."

"Not on your life," Uncle Lath agreed. "We can only hope they have found her—in time." He had to admit that in the short time he had known Gentle Lamb, he too had come to love the child. She was as endearing as a newborn kitten.

"We have to go help them find her," Led begged. "I know where she hides. I will go along."

"There isn't any point in going tonight," Arnold said. The three uncles nodded in agreement. "It is already dark, and that storm out there would see us all dead before morning."

"You might as well all stay here," Mrs. Bowen offered. They did have a big house, and there was plenty of space for them. "That way, if the weather lets up you can strike out first thing in the morning."

It was quickly agreed, and they all retired for the night, but they did not sleep.

As soon as the first rays of morning light hit the windows, the men were up and raring to go. Mrs. Bowen fixed them a good hot breakfast and took her heavy winter coat from the hook by the back door.

"What do you think you are doing?" Arnold asked.

"I'm going too," she said, tying her woolen bonnet on, "and don't you try to stop me. If we get to where we see tracks from them, there is only one way to make them hear us." She put two fingers into her mouth and let loose with the most blood-curdling whistle you ever heard.

"Can't argue with that," Uncle King said, laughing.

"Nope," Uncle Lath concurred.

"Let's get going," Uncle Lon said.

They went out to the barn, plowing their way through the thick wet snow. At least the sun was out and the wind and snow had stopped. With any luck at all they would find the missing party soon. If only, they all thought, it is in time to keep Gentle Lamb from doing something stupid.

"Go that way," Led said, pointing to a distant cave. "There's a cave there where she hides a lot. It is one of her favorite places."

They steered the horses in that direction. "Please, let her be safe," Mrs. Bowen prayed silently.

~*~

Violet and Denis rode slowly along the edge of the bluffs, calling "Gentle Lamb!" as they went. Before long they spotted tiny footprints in the snow. They came out of one of the caves, circled around, then went back inside.

They pulled the horse inside, dismounted and ran deep inside, calling to her as they ran. They found her, curled up in a corner, shivering violently from the cold.

Denis reached down and scooped her into his arms.

"You scared us to death!" he said, hugging her so tightly to his body she felt like she was being crushed. "Why did you run away?"

Tears filled her big dark, round eyes. "It was all my fault," she sobbed.

"What are you talking about?" Violet asked, rubbing her thick black hair as she spoke.

"The people in town," Gentle Lamb said. "They don't want me at the school. I—I heard them."

"How?" Violet asked.

"I was outside the window, listening. I heard them fighting about me. Then I saw you fighting with each other. I—I saw you push her." She looked accusingly at Denis, her eyes filled with terror.

Violet's heart went out to her. She knew she had watched her grandfather abuse her mother and her grandmother. No wonder she was frightened.

181

"Denis and I were just playing," Violet said, trying to exp̤.
to her. "We were worried about you too. You were so—far away
from us. We tried to reach out to you, but you wouldn't let us."

"We love you," Denis said, wrapping his arms of steel even
tighter around her. "We would never let anything bad happen to
you."

"And the people in town agreed to let you attend school," Violet
said. "They are proud to have you."

"But why?" Gentle Lamb asked.

"Because of Denis," Violet said. "You heard what he told them?"

"No," she said. "I just heard them fighting. I ran back home
before anybody saw me. I was afraid of what they might do to me.
What did he say?"

"It doesn't matter," Denis said, giving Violet a warning glance.
She didn't need any more guilt for what her people had done or
the way they had been treated. They were, he thought, recalling
Violet's words to him the first night she had arrived, "just people
too."

"But I saw you push her," she said to Denis.

"I didn't push her hard enough to hurt her," he said. "I would
never hurt her."

Denis turned to Violet, smiled and said, "If you think it could
be arranged, I would like to ask for your hand in marriage."

She was taken aback. Even after last night, she never expected
this.

"Why?" she asked somewhat sarcastically. "Because you have
made me a wanton woman? Your mistress?"

"No, silly," he said, tweaking her little button nose. He did not
dare tell her how close he had come last night in the cave to doing
his best to make that true. "You will never be a wanton woman.
Wanted, yes, by me, but wanton, never! Because I love you."

Gentle Lamb watched the two of them. She didn't understand
what they were saying at all. English was such a dumb language.
It didn't make sense half the time.

"Yes," Violet said, her heart soaring to the tops of the bluffs.
"Yes, yes, yes!"

Gentle Lamb's eyes lit up like the northern star on a clear winter
night.

"And you will be our own little girl," Denis said. "I will go talk to Black Cloud about it as soon as we get back to town."

Denis lifted Violet onto the horse, mounted himself in front of her, then lifted Gentle Lamb up in front of him. Slowly they walked towards the cave opening. They all ducked their heads low as they went outside.

~*~

From off in the distance the sound of hoofbeats echoed through the air. As it got closer, Gentle Lamb cried out, "No! It is Black Cloud! He will—he will kill me!"

"I will protect you," Denis said, trying to reassure her, but he knew he was no match for Black Cloud, especially not if he was angry.

When he spotted them, Black Cloud called out in Sioux, "I come in peace."

Denis told Violet what he said. Violet asked, "How do we know we can trust him?"

Gentle Lamb understood Violet's words, but in the midst of her fear she was much more comfortable conversing with Denis in her native tongue.

Denis quickly translated for Violet. "She says her grandfather is many things, but he always speaks the truth. If he says he comes in peace, he will do us no harm."

In no time at all Black Cloud sat on his mighty horse directly in front of them.

"I heard you had run away," he said, pulling closer to the trio on their horse. As he got close enough to touch them, his eyes focused on Gentle Lamb's necklace. He reached out and ran his fingers slowly over it. Denis's arms went out around her as she sat in front of him on his horse.

Gentle Lamb pushed Black Cloud's hand away from her necklace, afraid he was going to jerk it off and take it away from her. She couldn't let that happen. It was all she had left of Little Flower, and she knew that her sister's spirit lived on in her—as long as she had the medicine wheel.

"You can't have it. It's mine," Gentle Lamb informed him.

"Wikpeyapi?" Black Cloud asked. "From Little Flower?"

"Yes," Gentle Lamb told him. "Her spirit lives."

"In you?" Black Cloud asked.

Soon Black Cloud and Gentle Lamb were buried deeply in a verbal exchange that left the little girl smiling warmly and the old chief looking like he was ready to cry.

Violet, seated behind Denis on his horse, felt like an outsider, intruding, yearning with everything within her to know what they were saying, but afraid to ask.

After some time, Denis lifted Gentle Lamb from their crowded horse to Black Cloud, who had his arms outstretched to receive her. Violet gasped.

"What are you doing?" she demanded.

"Black Cloud has asked to take her back home with him. He says she belongs with her own people."

"But he will surely abuse her."

"No," Denis said, then sat there, silent, like that should be the end of the discussion.

"I don't understand," Violet said.

"He said he is sorry," Denis said. He knew it would be hard to make Violet understand. She didn't really know their ways yet, although she was trying hard to learn.

"Indian men almost never admit they are wrong," Denis continued, "and never the chief. He is almost a god to their people."

"But why?" Violet asked. "What changed his mind?"

"The wikpeyapi," Denis said. "The giveaway. He said he felt Little Flower's spirit as soon as he approached us, even before he saw it. That is why he said he came in peace. He said he knew he had been wrong."

Violet cried—long hard sobs. Denis slid off his horse and moved her forward, then he remounted behind her. He wrapped his arms lovingly around her, nuzzling his nose in her hair. Eventually she stopped crying.

"I'm sure she will be just fine," Denis said confidently. Somehow, watching the expressions on Black Cloud's face as he talked to Gentle Lamb, he knew that he would not mistreat her again. He hoped the same would hold true for Rose Petal.

"But I will miss her terribly," Violet said.

"She asked him if she could visit you. He agreed that she can."

Violet smiled. "That's good," she said.

"He also said that she—and the other Indian children—can attend your school."

Violet was nearly speechless. Finally she asked, "Are you certain? You didn't misunderstand him, did you?"

"Of course I'm certain," he said, feigning a hurt ego by grasping his heart. "Didn't I tell you that I am good at many things?"

Sitting in front of him, Violet couldn't see his face, but she knew he was grinning.

~*~

"Look!" Led shouted. "There they are!"

"We passed Black Cloud and Gentle Lamb a ways back," Arnold said. "Led said they had made peace. Can it be?"

"Yes," Denis said. "He seemed quite sincere."

"That is wonderful," Mrs. Bowen said. "So are you two youngsters ready to go home?"

"Youngsters?" Denis said. "I'm quite old enough to..."

"To what?" Arnold asked, frustrated at being left dangling.

"To take a bride," Denis said, his voice filled with glee.

Arnold grinned from ear to ear. "Looks like Sugar Loaf worked its magic once more," he said.

They all nodded knowingly. Mrs. Bowen reached under her and pulled an extra blanket that she had brought along and handed it to Violet, who took off Denis's leather jacket and wrapped the blanket around herself and wondered how long it would take before she could stop shivering.

Mrs. Bowen let out one of her famous whistles, calling to the horses, signaling them to turn around and head back to Lake City. Denis's horse bolted, but soon followed behind them.

"That should let the uncles know we found them," Arnold said as he laughed heartily.

"The three uncles," Mrs. Bowen said, joining in the laughter. "If they were smarter we could call them 'The Three Wisemen.'"

~*~

"She's so tiny," Violet said, talking about Mrs. Bowen as they watched them loom ahead of them.

"But she packs one gigantic punch," Denis said as he applied pressure with his boots to the horse's side so they could catch up with the Bowens.

"Yes, Blackie, I think the magic is done. Come on, let's go home."

Violet turned back to look at the bluffs. Even in the snow, they were magic. Softly, almost silently, she said "Thank you" to them. Life in Paradise was indeed going to be perfect.

A Note from the Author

I love it when I read a book and the geographical setting is as much a part of the story as the characters themselves. I hope that will be the case with Maiden Rock Mistress for the readers. You see, Lake City, Minnesota and Maiden Rock, Wisconsin both hold a very special place in my heart.

My mother was born and raised in Lake City. As a youngster, I spent a lot of time there. One of my favorite things to do was to go up to the bluffs on Sugar Loaf with my Great Uncle Glen Bowen. The sand was all different colors, as it is described in the book. How sad that now, many years later, the beautiful multi-colored sand has disappeared. It has, I suppose, been hauled away and put in all those jars that used to sit on the window ledges or by tourists. It reminded me, as I was writing this book, that we need to be good stewards of our land. We hear so much about protecting our environment, but it never really hit home with me until I pondered this very personal attack on something that I had cherished for so many years. It makes me much more conscious of what I do and how I treat the things around me that we so often take for granted. I hope it will do the same for all of you.

Maiden Rock, Wisconsin was the home of my late husband Ivan's Smith family. Almost thirty years ago I began to trace our family tree, beginning with his Keith family. (You can read all about them in my Keith Trilogy: Dunnottar, Marylebone and Par for the Course.) It was only after learning that his great-grandfather, Josiah King Smith, served in the Civil War and getting his military papers from the National Archive that we discovered that the Keiths and the Smiths from his family all lived in Lake

City too. In fact, many of them are buried just a few families apart in the cemetery there.

Also, I enjoy drawing on my own family for my stories. I have had many readers ask me which of my characters are real and which ones are fictional. There is a mix of them in Maiden Rock Mistress. I will leave it up to you, the readers, to try to determine which is which. If, after you have read the book, you want to send me your guesses on it, I will let you know how close you came.

Nothing is more fun for an author than hearing from our "fans." Please feel free to contact me at janetelainesmith@yahoo.com, P.O. Box 264, Amberg WI 54102, or through my website at http://www.janetelainesmith.com.

I hope you enjoy a glimpse into a very special place in my heart as you travel with me through Maiden Rock Mistress.

With love and appreciation,

Janet Elaine Smith

Printed in the United States
218848BV00002B/9/P

9 781935 188056